Marion Lennox has written over one hundred romance novels, and is published in over one hundred countries and thirty languages. Her international awards include the prestigious RITA® award (twice!) and the *RT Book Reviews* Career Achievement Award for 'a body of work which makes us laugh and teaches us about love'. Marion adores her family, her kayak, her dog, and lying on the beach with a book someone else has written. Heaven!

SECOND CHANCE WITH HER ISLAND DOC

MARION LENNOX

MILLS & BOON

First published in Great Britain 2019
by Mills & Boon, an imprint of HarperCollins*Publishers*
1 London Bridge Street, London, SE1 9GF

Large Print edition 2020

© 2019 Marion Lennox

ISBN: 978-0-263-08544-0

FLINTSHIRE SIR Y FFLINT	
C29 0000 1223 767	
ULV	£16.99

certified
gement. For
.uk/green.

4YY

CHAPTER ONE

'HEAD LACERATIONS ALWAYS look worse than they are. If you'll help me to a washbasin I'll stop wasting your time. I'm not dizzy any more. Really.'

The woman's voice drifting from the treatment room was warm, husky and a little bit shaky. She was speaking the Tovahnan language, with an English accent overlaid.

Dr Leo Aretino knew this voice well. For the last few weeks he'd been expecting her arrival on the island, but hoping he could avoid her.

He hadn't been expecting her here, in his territory.

The language she was speaking was Leo's native tongue. The first time he'd heard her use it had been over ten years ago. She'd been standing over a microscope, trying to focus. The 'scope had been fiddly, but Anna had been patient. She'd started humming, and then softly singing to herself. In Tovahnan.

It was a tune his mother had taught him as a child.

Leo had doubted if anyone at their prestigious English medical school had even heard of his birthplace, the island of Tovahna, much less known how to speak its language. He'd cut across her song, incredulous. 'Where did you learn that?'

'From my mother,' she'd said. She'd had the slide in focus at that point and had been looking intently at the nasty little pathogen the tutor wanted them to see.

'Your mother's Tovahnan?'

'Yes, she is. Or she was. She left Tovahna before I was born.' Anna had checked the slide again. 'But it's this little guy we're interested in. You want to look?'

There was a queue. He needed to look at the bug.

His attention was solidly diverted.

Tovahna was a Mediterranean island, sparsely populated, fought over for centuries until its big neighbours had decided it wasn't worth the bother. It was now mostly ignored by the outside world. Few foreigners made the effort to visit, much less learn the language. The women of

Tovahna were generally olive skinned and dark haired. Anna had red hair and freckles. This didn't make sense.

'Your mother taught you Tovahnan songs?'

'She taught me the language.' She'd moved away from the microscope, allowing the student after Leo access. 'I think she used it to assuage homesickness. But you've missed your turn,' she'd told him, switching effortlessly into speaking Tovahnan. She'd smiled, a wide, happy smile that had made him feel even more astounded. 'Don't tell me you're...'

'Tovahnan.' And suddenly he'd been close to tears.

Tovahna was tiny, impoverished, its assets gouged for generations by a single family dynasty. Most of its people were trapped in a ceaseless cycle of poverty, but Leo had been so smart at school that the community had rallied to send him to England.

'Get yourself a medical degree and then come home and help us,' they'd told him, and off he'd gone, aged all of fifteen.

At nineteen he'd been doing brilliantly. His English had been flawless. He'd fitted in with his fellow students. He'd even been enjoying himself, hardly homesick at all. So there'd been no reason why he should gaze at this redheaded, freckled, fellow student speaking his language and feel like…he'd wanted to take her into his arms.

Of course, he hadn't. Not right then. It had been two whole days before he'd kissed her.

It wasn't just that they'd shared a language. Anna had been special.

But that was past history, he told himself as he listened to her voice carrying from the next room. What was between them had been a long time ago. Right now he needed to focus on medical imperatives. A woman he'd met years before was being carried into his emergency room on a stretcher.

He was a doctor and he had to deal with whoever needed to be treated. He needed to haul himself together and go see what the problem was.

The medical problem.

Wow, her head hurt.

The thump against stone had been stupid and entirely predictable. When she'd insisted she wanted to see everything—she now owned a castle and who wouldn't want to see it all?—her late cousin's agent had given her a torch.

'Watch your head,' he'd told her as he'd led her deep into the depths of Tovahna Castle.

What she'd seen had been a maze of tunnels, some built almost a thousand years ago. Secret passages led in and out from the castle walls, to be used in times of siege. There were hidden living areas, ventilation shafts, storage spaces for weapons, for food and water, all dark and dusty and so fascinating it was no wonder she'd finally forgotten to watch her head.

The thump had been solid and the results immediate. The world had spun and then disappeared. She'd surfaced to find blood oozing down her forehead. Victoir, the agent, had been useless, torn between wanting to help and not wanting to get blood on his suit. Finally she'd ripped off her windcheater and applied pressure herself, then had him help her to the surface.

'I don't want paramedics coming down here,' she'd told him. 'This looks worse than it is. You'll have a team of split heads instead of one.'

But emerging to daylight, Victoir's authority reasserted itself. 'I've called the ambulance,' he told her. 'I said those passages were dangerous. They need to be closed off, filled in, before someone's killed. Kids get in and we can't stop them. You've seen the parts that are crumbling. And now this...'

And then a rattletrap ambulance had come blaring down the cobblestoned street to the castle forecourt, and Anna had been bundled inside before she could object.

She could hardly blame them, she decided. She probably did look like something out of *The Texas Chainsaw Massacre*, and, to be honest, she was still a bit woozy. So she'd lain back and let the paramedics put in a drip to compensate for blood loss. She'd felt every bumpy cobble as they'd made their way who knew where, until finally she'd been carried into what looked a plain, businesslike emergency entrance.

'The doctor's on his way,' a middle-aged nurse told her. She didn't attempt to remove the windcheater-pad Anna was still holding. 'Don't worry. Our Dr Leo's on duty and he's the best we have.'

And her bad day suddenly got worse.

Dr Leo. No! Please...

But then the door swung open and a guy in a white coat was beside her trolley. 'Maria, what do we have here?'

And her worst fears were realised.

Leo Aretino. Her first love.

Her greatest love.

How could you be truly in love at nineteen? You couldn't be, she'd decided. What they'd had had been a teenage fling.

He'd broken her heart, but teenagers' hearts were made to be broken. She'd told herself that over and over in the years between then and now. She'd met other men. She'd even fancied herself in love with them, but the thought of Leo had always stayed with her. Tall, dark, intense, speaking the language of her mother, making her laugh, studying with her, making her body sing...

And then walking away...

She closed her eyes. Her head felt like it was about to explode and it wasn't just the pain from the accident.

She'd guessed she might meet him when she came here, but to meet him now, like this...

'It's Anna Raymond.' The nurse's voice held suppressed excitement. 'Anna Castlavara. Katrina's daughter. Victoir was showing her the tunnels under the castle.'

'Of course.' Leo's voice was smooth, unfussed,

as if the name meant nothing to him. Had he known she'd be in the country? He must have, she thought. For Tovahna this must have been big news.

It had been big news to her. Her cousin's death. An inheritance so huge she could hardly take it in.

Leo.

'Anna and I have met before.' Leo still sounded calm. Professional. Like she was one of the scores of patients he saw each day. She was a fellow student he'd had a casual fling with ten years ago. No more.

A fellow student who'd inherited most of his country?

'Anna.' His voice gentled and he spoke in English. 'Are you with us?'

'I'm with you.' She couldn't keep ten years of resentment from her voice. 'Unfortunately.'

'Can you open your eyes?'

'I can but I don't want to.'

'Because the light hurts?'

'Because I don't want to see you.'

And the man had the temerity to chuckle.

'Still the firebrand I remember, then, Anna?

Okay, keep those eyes closed and I'll check out the rest.'

His hand was on her wrist and the touch made her...what? She should want to pull away.

She didn't do that either.

He didn't touch the pad on her head. He was doing an overall assessment, she thought, checking the IV line, blood pressure, the paramedic notes. Taking in the whole picture.

He was a fine doctor. She remembered that comment at their graduation ceremony. Leo hadn't been there. As soon as his last exam was behind him he'd left to do a fast track course in surgery before heading home. To Tovahna. But at the graduation his name had been read out with pride by the head of the medical faculty. 'Dr Leo Aretino has topped almost every class during his time here and he intends returning to serve his country. He's a doctor we can be proud of, now and into the future.'

So she was in good hands. Leo's hands.

She hurt.

'Is it just your head?' The laughter was gone now—he was all doctor—and that gentle voice she remembered so well was almost enough to bring tears to her eyes. 'Anna, have you hurt anything else?'

'Just m-my head,' she managed, and was ashamed it came out as a stammered whisper.

'Do you remember what happened?'

'There was a cavern with ancient pottery urns. I bent to see and then stood up.' She managed to dredge up a bit of indignation but it was directed at herself. 'Victoir said it was dangerous and I didn't listen.'

'The notes said you lost consciousness.'

'Victoir said I was out of it for a few seconds, but all I can remember is *bang* and then feeling dizzy.'

Leo would be thinking of internal bleeding, she thought. Did they have the facilities to treat that here?

She'd read about Tovahna over the years—of course she had.

Still almost a feudal economy, with one family controlling much of the wealth. Most of the population pay rent to the Castlavaran family, and little is put back into infrastructure. Schools, hospitals, public services are minimal, to say the least.

Tourist sites reported on the medical facilities, too.

Travellers are advised to carry extra health insurance to cover transport to a neighbouring country. Medical services are basic. Complex medical situations often mean either evacuation or a less than satisfactory outcome.

A less than satisfactory outcome. Death?

'If I did lose consciousness it was only for seconds,' she said, more surely now. Wanting to reassure herself as well as him. 'You know split heads bleed enough to make people think you're at death's door.'

'Blood running down faces does seem to frighten onlookers,' he agreed, and she heard the hint of humour return. It was the laughter she'd fallen for. *Oh, Leo...* 'We'll take X-rays to be sure, though.'

'You have facilities?'

'Amazingly, we have.' The laughter was still there, but underneath...the trace of bitterness she'd heard only once but would remember for ever. Old accusations flooded back. *'Your family has sucked our country dry...'*

'I'm sorry. I didn't mean...'

'Let's take a look,' he said, gentle again, and he moved the padded windcheater aside.

The paramedics had moved it to do a fast check but they'd replaced it and bound it fast, thinking it was best not to disturb things until they had a doctor's back-up. Now the bleeding had stopped, and it had become sticky. She felt the windcheater tug on the dried blood in her hair.

She had no choice. Finally she opened her eyes.

Leo was right there, leaning over her. His face was maybe two hand widths from hers. This was a Leo who was older, his face creased a little, with age, with weather, his eyes seemingly deeper set.

But he was the same Leo. Those gorgeous brown eyes. The deep black, crinkly hair, a bit unkempt. The laughter lines. His mouth…

It was as if he was about to kiss…

Um…not. He was looking at her head, not into her eyes.

Oh, but those eyes…

She needed to get over herself.

She'd never intended seeing him. Once she'd got over the shock of her inheritance, her intention had been to come here fast, put the organisation of the estate firmly back into the hands of her cousin's agent and then retreat. She knew the country was impoverished and she had no intention of making it more so. Her uncle and then her cousin had squirrelled away rents and profits. She needed to figure a way to channel them into charities, and then go home.

Home was in England, where she worked as a family doctor in a village a couple of hours south of London. The community was lovely and she loved her job. She had two beloved springer spaniels, dopy but fun. She'd recently broken up with a rather nice lawyer but they were still friends. She had lots of friends. Life was good.

This inheritance had been like a bombshell. Now, looking up into Leo's face, it seemed even more so.

For the reason things had never progressed with her 'rather nice lawyer' was right here. After all this time, to have this memory messing with her life...

This memory? Leo.

But Leo wasn't looking at her. His fingers—oh, she remembered those fingers—were carefully untangling the matted hair so he could see what he was dealing with.

'This was some thump,' he told her. 'You'll

need stitches and a thorough check. Sorry, Anna, but we need to shave some of your hair.'

'Nothing a scarf won't hide,' she said, trying for lightness. 'It was my own fault.'

'But you *were* down in the underground labyrinth.'

'Just checking.'

'Checking your inheritance.'

'That's right.' How hard was that to say lightly?

'I'm sorry about your cousin.'

'Really?' She was trying not to wince at the feel of his fingers. Not from pain, though. He was being gentle.

He always had been gentle.

'Yanni's death was unexpected,' he told her, still carefully probing. 'Although with the lifestyle he led…'

'Eating and hoarding money,' she said. 'I've been told. My mother said his father—Mum's brother—was the same.'

'And he died of a heart attack as well,' Leo said. 'Twenty years apart, both their deaths almost instant. Your cousin was only thirty-eight, but with the lifestyle he led and his family history… There was nothing we could do.'

'Hey, I'm not blaming you.' She sighed. Her

head really did hurt. 'Leo, could you find someone else to stitch my head? To be honest, having you treating me is making me feel a whole lot worse. You don't like anything about me and my family, right?'

'I treated your cousin,' he said, without answering her question. 'Or I tried to. He refused to listen to concerns about cholesterol or weight. But I did my best. I'll do my best with you.'

'You can't imagine how grateful that makes me feel,' she muttered. 'Is there no one else?'

'Not right now. Our only other doctor is in the midst of a birth.'

'You only have two doctors?'

'This island's small.'

'I've read about it. Twenty thousand people. Two doctors?'

'You tell me how to get the money to train them and I'll do something about it. We have a couple of islanders we've trained as nurse-practitioners. They're good, but for a head wound you need either Carla or me.'

She'd known the island was impoverished. Two doctors, though, for such a population... Now, though, wasn't the time for thinking about it. 'I'll wait for Carla,' she said, and she knew she sounded belligerent but she couldn't help it. This man had hurt her in the past and hurt her badly. She didn't want him anywhere near her.

'I doubt if you can wait that long.' He stood back a little, studying her. Like an interesting bug? Like he didn't even know her. 'So what were you doing climbing under the castle without a hard hat?'

'A hard hat...' she said cautiously, and thought about it. Or tried to think about it. The knock had made her feel ill, and Leo's presence was now removing almost all the rest of her ability to think logically. 'Maybe that would have been sensible,' she conceded at last. 'It wasn't offered as an option, though, and I really wanted to see.'

'So Victoir took you underground?'

'He was my cousin's agent. He knows the place.'

'He also knows the rule about hard hats. He didn't warn you?'

'Of course he did. He said it's dangerous. He said the entire underground needs to be closed off, and I guess now I agree. My inheritance states that capital must be used to improve or maintain the castle itself. That's pretty limiting. Victoir's idea is that I close off the underground area and divide the castle into apartments. He says with the view over the sea they'll command exorbitant rent and provide an economic boost for the whole island.'

'I imagine they will,' Leo said dryly. 'And an economic boost for Victoir as well. So he told you that going underground was dangerous.'

'I told you.' She sighed. 'Leo, can we just get on with this? Fix my head, charge me what you like and let me go.'

'You know I won't keep you longer than I must,' he said, formally now. 'But losing consciousness… You know as well as I do that overnight obs are essential. Like it or not, you're stuck here for the night.'

He turned back to the nurse, switching back into Tovahnan. 'Maria, let's get this X-rayed before we do a proper clean-up,' he told her. 'Can you take her through? I'll get some pain relief in first, though.' He turned back to Anna. 'Pain… One to ten?'

She thought about it and decided to be honest. Her head was thumping.

'Maybe…six?'

'Ouch,' he said, sympathetically. 'You do need

that X-ray. But a nice shot of something first. Any allergies?'

'None.' What he said made sense. 'Thank you,' she said, and was annoyed at how feeble she sounded.

And astonishingly he touched her hand, lightly. It was the kind of touch he might give any patient he wanted to reassure. It was entirely professional, so why it seemed to burn...

It didn't. She was being dumb. This kind of thump on her head would make anyone dumb, she told herself. He was being purely professional. 'Right, let's get you sorted. Maria can take X-rays. I'll come back with the results as soon as I can.'

'Thank you,' she managed. 'There's no hurry.'

'There's always a hurry,' he said, and suddenly it was a snap. 'That's what my life is, thanks to your family.'

Your family... The words resonated, an echo of what he'd said all those years ago.

'Your family robs my country blind, leeching every asset we ever had. How can I associate myself with anyone even remotely connected to the Castlavarans? I'm sorry, it's over, Anna.'

'So the judgement's still there,' she managed,

and stupidly she was starting to feel her eyes well with unshed tears. It was the shock, she told herself. A decent thump on the head always messed with the tear ducts.

It wasn't anything to do with this arrogant, judgemental guy she'd once loved with all her heart.

'It's not judgement, it's knowledge,' he told her. 'Maria will take care of you. I'll be back to sew things up. By the way, I will be charging.'

'Charge what you like,' she muttered. 'And get me out of here as soon as possible. All I want to do is go home.'

He wanted her out of here as much as she wanted to be gone. Maybe more. The thought of a Castlavaran in his treatment room should be enough to make his skin crawl.

Only this was Anna, and what he felt for her...

She was two parts, he conceded. She was Anna Raymond, the redheaded, gorgeous, fun-loving fellow student he'd fallen in love with. But she was still Anna Castlavara, daughter of Katrina Castlavara, who was in turn the daughter of a family who'd held the wealth of this small country in its grasping hands for generations.

'They're nothing to do with me.'

He remembered Anna's response when he'd first discovered the connection. His reaction had been guttural, instinctive, incredulous. For six months he'd been dating her. He'd been nineteen, a student madly in love, thinking life was as good as it could get. And then he'd met her mother.

Katrina had been in America when he'd first met Anna, with a guy Anna had said was one of a string of men.

'We hardly see each other,' she'd told him, but she'd told him little else.

It seemed she'd known little.

'As far as I know, she left Tovahna in her teens and she hasn't been back. She said her mother died young and her father's horrible, but that's pretty much all she'll tell me. I imagine Mum would have been a wild child, so maybe that had something to do with it. Sometimes, though... when I was little she'd sing to me, songs like the one you heard, and in between men, when she was bored, she taught me Tovahnan. It's always seemed fun, our own secret language. I suspect she was a bit homesick, though she'd never admit it. She refuses to talk of her

family—she says they've rejected her and she's rejected them. She's said there's no way she'd ever go back—that most of the young people from Tovahna end up emigrating.'

They still did, Leo thought grimly. The extent of economic activity on the island was to grow olives and tomatoes, fish and pay exorbitant rents to the Castlavaran landlords.

There'd never been a king, a president, even an official ruler. The island was simply owned by the Castlavarans. For generation after generation they had ruled with a grasping hand and nothing had disturbed that rule. There was little on this rocky island to invite invasion. Its inhabitants were peaceful, ultra-conservative, accepting the status quo because that's what their parents had, and their parents before them.

Right now, though, the status quo had changed. The last male heir, Yanni, had left no descendants. The inheritance had thus fallen to a woman the country didn't know, a woman who'd been born abroad, a woman who—as far as Leo could tell—knew little about her ancestors' homeland.

Was it time for the population to rise up and say, 'Enough'? The land should be owned by the people who'd worked it for generations.

It wasn't happening. Any kid with any ambition had one thought and that was to emigrate, and the remaining islanders accepted apathy as the norm. That meant that Anna's inheritance was being met with stoic acceptance.

Maybe he should lead a revolution himself, but he was far too busy to think of political insurrection. Work was always waiting.

Like Anna's split head.

'Please let it not be fractured,' he muttered as he left her. Not only for her sake either. He needed to get her out of his hospital and then get on with his life.

His next patient was a child brought in by his grandparents 'because he won't eat', which probably meant he'd been given so many sweets he didn't need anything else. But they'd been waiting for over three hours. The toddler's parents were off the island, visiting the little boy's ill maternal grandmother, and he didn't want them worried, so he took the time to reassure the grandparents. He gave them a chart where every single thing that went into the small boy's mouth had to be recorded, no matter what, and sent them away dubious. But if they stuck to the chart they'd have forty fits when they saw how much they were sneaking—behind each other's backs—into one small mouth.

At any other time that might have made him smile, but he wasn't smiling when he returned to check Anna's X-rays.

All okay. Excellent.

He still had to keep her in overnight. There remained a risk of internal bleeding.

But first stitching.

Carla was still caught up with a tricky birth. He checked in, hopeful, but there was no joy there.

'She may need a Caesarean,' Carla told him. Carla was in her sixties, tough and practical and kind. 'We're doing the best we can. First sign of foetal distress, though, and I'll need you. Don't go anywhere, Leo.'

'I was wondering if you could do a stitching,' he told her, glancing behind her to the woman in labour. 'Swap places?'

'I've been with Greta all the way,' Carla said. 'It's not kind to swap now.' And then she grinned. 'Besides, Maria tells me she's the Castlavara. I understand why you want to swap. Just treat her like anyone else and then multiply the costs by a hundred. Hey, if you're nice to her maybe we could persuade her to fund us a new ambulance. Put on your charm, Dr Aretino, and go charm yourself our future.'

To say she was miserable was an understatement. She was tucked into a cubicle with curtains around her, cut off from the outside world. The painkiller Leo had prescribed had taken effect but was causing even more fuzziness, and there was still a dull ache. She was in a foreign country, in the hands of a man who'd made it clear ten years ago that he was rejecting her.

She wanted to go home so badly she could taste it, to her lovely little cottage in her English village, to people who treated her as a friend as well as a doctor, to her two happy, bouncy dogs.

It was mid-afternoon. Rhonda, her next-door neighbour, would be walking her dogs, letting them roam in the woods behind her cottage. The dogs would be going nuts, exploring the springtime smells, chasing rabbits, chasing each other, free…

Oh, for heaven's sake, she was close to tears again and she never cried. She was an independent, strong career woman and tears were dumb. How she was feeling was dumb.

She should have asked someone to come with her. Her ex-boyfriend? Martin was a lawyer. They'd had what could only be called a tepid relationship before he'd fallen madly, deeply for her best friend, Jennifer. But they'd stayed friends and when the news of her inheritance had come through both he and Jennifer had been fascinated.

'Summary,' Martin had announced after considerable research. 'The estate's tied up in such a way you can't offload it and the country's in a mess. That mess is not of your making, though, and the Trust doesn't give you much option to do anything about it. My advice? Leave it in the hands of this Victoir guy, who knows the layout. It's pulling in an incredible income. Yes, the settlement decrees most of the income stays with the castle, but as overall owner you're entitled to living expenses and those living expenses can be more than generous. You'll be set for life. Sign the papers and forget about the rest.'

But it seemed too big, too huge, to simply sign and forget. Her colleagues were intrigued and helpful. Rhonda was happy to take care of the dogs.

There was the long-ago memory of a boy called

Leo, but Tovahna was surely not so small she'd bump into him in the street.

So she'd bumped into a twelfth-century stone ceiling and she'd found Leo all by herself.

Oh, her head hurt.

And then Leo was back, brisk, formal, hurried. 'Okay, Anna, let's get these stitches sorted. Your X-rays are clear. No fractures. We'll need to keep you in overnight for obs—you know that—but there should be no problem. Maria's bringing what we need now.'

She hadn't heard footsteps. She hadn't heard the curtain draw back. Leo was just…here.

Her head felt like it might explode.

If she'd had a few seconds' warning, if she'd heard him approach, then maybe she could have kept control, but she hadn't and she didn't. She made a desperate grab for the tissue box on the side table and buried her face in a sea of white.

Heroines in movies cried beautifully, glistening droplets slipping silently down beautifully made-up faces, lips quivering as brave heroines fought back overwhelming sadness. Then they'd blink back remaining tears and gaze adoringly at their hero with eyes still misty, and…*most infuriating of all*…not a hint of puffiness in sight.

Then there'd be a kiss, with the heroine not even needing to sniff.

But that was in movie land, not on an examination trolley in a sterile, strange emergency room. Anna had to sniff. More, she had to blow her nose and even when she blew it, it kept running. And blinking was useless with this flood. Her shoulders were shaking with silent sobs and she couldn't stop them.

This was crazy.

But maybe she should cut herself some slack.

She'd hardly slept since she'd received the news last week. The journey here had been arduous—where were decent connections when you needed them? Victoir had bombarded her with information she'd had no hope of getting her head around but she knew she had to. And then the dark, the bang, the shock and the loss of blood. She was overtired, overwrought, drugged and still in pain. And finally here was Leo, looking at her like she was something the cat had dragged in.

Leo, whom she'd once loved with all her heart.

She was buried under a wad of tissues but she needed more. She made a desperate swipe for the box but she didn't connect.

And then a wad of dry tissues was tucked into her hand. The sodden ones were removed.

She could hardly thank him. She blew her nose again and struggled to stop the stupid tears.

Everything was shaking.

Stupid drugs. Stupid head. Stupid, stupid, stupid...

And then there was a heavy sigh and she felt a weight on the side of her bed. And arms came around her and gathered her into a warm, strong hug.

It needed only this.

The sensible part of Anna should react with horror. Sensible Anna should shove him away, tell him to take his prejudiced, judgemental self anywhere but here. The sensible part of Anna would...what? Walk out of here, bloodstained and woozy. Call Victoir to come get her?

But right now the sensible part of Anna wasn't big enough to mount a coherent argument. The rest of her was mush, and that mush was being held fast by arms she knew.

She was being held against a chest she loved.

She didn't love. She didn't! But right now she needed. She let herself fold against him, feeling the strength of his arms, the warmth, the solidness.

He was wearing a clinical coat, a bit stiff. It felt okay. More, it felt good. Medicine and Leo, they were a solid combination of safety, surety. Home...

Where had that word come from? Home was England, the dogs, her village, her people.

She could feel his heart beating. Strong. Steady. Leo.

The shaking was easing. Whatever was happening, this helped. She had no strength to draw away and she didn't want to. Drug-free medicine... A hug...

She let her mind stop its useless spinning and focus on just being held.

By Leo.

There was no pressure. He didn't push her away, even as her sobs subsided. He simply sat and held her, letting her take as much time as she needed to get herself back together.

Letting her take as much comfort as she needed.

And she did need it. She didn't want to draw back.

This was an illusion, a memory of times past,

a comfort that shouldn't be any kind of comfort at all.

Oh, but he felt...

'Dressing tray.' The female voice... Maria's?... came from the doorway. And then there was an apologetic reaction as the nurse saw what was happening. 'Whoops, sorry, back in a moment.'

'It's okay.' Finally—to her regret—Leo pulled back. 'Bring it in, Maria. Anna, are we all right to get these stitches in?'

'I... Of course.' The tears were gone. She was bloodstained, puffy-eyed and mortified, but somehow she hauled together what was left of her rag-tailed dignity. 'Stitches and then twelve hours of obs and I'm out of here.'

'That's what we both want,' Leo said, and, comfort or not, the old resentments surged back.

This man was her treating doctor. She needed him to help her. He'd comforted her with a hug.

She still wanted to slap him.

CHAPTER TWO

IT WAS A long night, and it wasn't just medical need that made it so.

The sweet-eating toddler and Anna's laceration were the last simple cases Leo saw. The birth Carla was attending did turn into a Caesarean and a dicey one at that. Greta was diabetic. She'd been desperate to have a natural delivery, had persuaded Carla to let her try, but by the time they'd bailed out her sugar levels had been all over the place. Carla took over the baby's care and Leo was left trying to stabilise mum.

Then there were three injured teens from a street brawl. It wasn't unusual. The kids here were bored. There were few jobs and little to aspire to.

And the woman responsible was in his hospital.

That wasn't fair, he conceded as the night wore on. He snatched a couple of hours' sleep but it was a disturbed rest, interspersed with thoughts of Anna. She hadn't personally been responsible for her family's greed.

But she was now. That one person could inherit such wealth, controlling the misery of so many lives… It made something inside him cold with fury, an anger he'd carried all his life.

Dawn saw him back on the wards. The teens were safe, their injuries relatively minor. Knife wounds, bruising, a couple of fractures, but he could cope with those. Ideally one of the boys should be sent to an orthopaedic surgeon, but where were the funds for that? He'd have to balance cost to the family against using the skills he had.

Breakfast was a fast cruise past the hospital kitchen. Carla found him there. She'd been home and slept. She was sixty but she usually chirped like she was about twenty years younger than Leo felt. This morning she was rubbing her temple, though, and looking tired.

'Headache?'

'I need aspirin,' she conceded. 'Though why I should have a headache when it's you who was up most of the night… Rough?'

He nodded, swigging lukewarm coffee. If there

was one thing he wanted more than anything it was to replace the coffee machine.

A new steriliser for Theatre came first. There were always things that came first.

'No deaths?' Carla queried, and he wondered if that was how he looked. Maybe. Anna's arrival had jolted his world.

'No one's dead,' he told her. 'Though there are three kids who tried. Knives, alcohol...' He shook his head. 'Seventeen years old and not a job or a prospect between them. It's a disaster, Carla.'

'So talk to the heiress.'

'You know the rules. The money's tied up in the castle. Even if I could persuade her...'

'You could try.'

'She's a Castlavaran. What's likely to change?' He swigged more coffee and put his mug aside. 'Ugh.'

'But she's an outsider.' Carla suddenly sounded chirpy again. 'And Maria says you've met her before.'

Of course. Nothing in this hospital went unnoticed.

'At medical school,' he said, brusquely. 'I didn't know who she was.'

'She's a doctor?'

'I imagine she finished her training, yes.'

'Wow. That's wonderful. You might even be able to persuade her to help us. Leo, what's needed here is charm.'

'Charm?' He eyed her with suspicion. He and Carla went back a long way. In fact, it had been a much younger Carla who'd persuaded Leo's mother—and the town—to send him to medical school in London. Carla herself had gone there, funded by an aunt who'd emigrated. She was full of energy and ideas and she wasn't afraid to speak her mind. He looked at her now and thought, Uh oh. He knew that look.

'Why not charm her?' she went on. 'Maybe even take it further. She's the same age as you are, and she owns practically this entire country. And now she's a doctor.'

'A doctor who's a Castlavaran.'

'That's prejudice,' she said sternly. 'I've a good mind to march in there and charm for myself.'

'You're welcome. She needs to be checked and discharged.'

'Your patient,' she said, and chuckled. 'And your project.'

'I have work to do. My plan is to get her out of here as soon as possible.'

'The country's stuck with her, though,' Carla said. 'You could put in a bit of effort.'

'Leave it,' he snapped, and then caught himself. Any minute now Carla would be sussing out past history. 'From all I gather, she's here to accept her inheritance and go.'

'So keep her in hospital a little longer.'

'Leave it, Carla,' he said again, and he heard his weariness reflected in his voice. 'We have work to do. Your headache...'

'Nothing aspirin can't fix,' Carla said, and she was watching him now with worry. She'd heard something in his voice. Seen something on his face? 'Leo, what's wrong with *you*?'

'Nothing that getting Anna out of our hospital won't fix. Let's move.'

Leo had written her up for painkillers, so Anna had slept. She'd had some breakfast. A very young nurse had helped her shower, washing away the worst of the bloodstains. She'd be wearing a scarf for a while but she was feeling a lot more in control.

She needed to get out of Leo's hospital.

Her tiny room was clean but shabby, with faded linoleum, a stark iron bedstead, a small wheeled table and nothing else. Its one high window looked out onto a brick wall and the light was from a single bulb, hanging high. It was hardly a room for feeling better in, she thought. It felt more like a cell.

Had Leo put her in here purposely? Was it the worst room he could find?

She wanted to leave, now.

Victoir turned up soon after breakfast with her suitcase. He was appalled—*appalled!*—by what had happened and his volubility made her tired. She persuaded him to disappear while she rid herself of the hospital gown, but the effort of tugging on jeans and T-shirt made her feel woozy. She settled back on the bed, and almost immediately Victoir reappeared, this time carrying a sheaf of documents so thick the ache in her head surged back.

'I can't read them here,' she told him. 'And I need legal advice if they're to do with the estate. Victoir, I'll take them back to England with me and get them checked.'

'I've only brought you the urgent ones,' he told her. 'These are things that can't wait. Like blocking those tunnels. I warned you. The sooner they're blocked—'

'The sooner you can start turning the castle into your dream apartments?'

The voice from the doorway made them both start. Leo. Of course it was. Victoir swivelled and scowled, and Anna flinched—which was stupid. She wasn't afraid of Leo.

She was afraid of how he made her feel.

'Good morning,' he said, edging into the tiny room. 'Victoir, can I ask you to leave while I check Ms Castlavara's condition?'

'I'm Anna Raymond,' she threw at him.

'You own the castle. This entire country knows you as the Castlavaran and I'm not about to argue with my country. Victoir...'

'Ms Raymond's about to sign some papers,' Victoir snapped. 'They're urgent.'

'More important than Anna's health?'

'What gives you the right to call her Anna?'

'I believe she gave me the right some years ago,' he said, meeting Victoir's challenge head on. 'When we met at medical school.'

What the...? Was Leo about to discuss their past history in front of Victoir? She felt herself go cold at the thought.

'We did meet while studying medicine,' she said, hurriedly and grudgingly. 'And he might as well use my first name if the alternative's Castlavara. Victoir, I'm sorry but I'm signing nothing now. Dr… Leo will tell you that I've been taking strong painkillers, so nothing I sign now will be legally binding anyway.'

'You're fine,' Victoir snapped. 'No one will argue.'

'I'll argue,' Leo said smoothly. 'Victoir, leave.'

'Please, Victoir,' Anna added. 'And take the papers with you. Honestly, I'm fuzzy.'

He knew when he was beaten. He cast her a look of frustration, but then softened.

'I'm sorry. You're right, you're in no condition to consider. But we'll get you home as soon as possible. You'll need a couple of days' recuperation—your castle accommodation will be a far cry from this.' And he cast the room a disgusted glance, Leo an angry one, and stalked out.

Leaving her with Leo, which left her feeling weird. Alone, vulnerable…scared?

'Don't you have a nurse accompany you on your rounds?' she asked, and for the life of her she couldn't stop herself sounding like some sort of sulky adolescent.

'If I was in England maybe I would,' he told her. 'But nurses cost money and this hospital has no money. We run on a skeleton staff. This whole country runs on a skeleton staff.'

It was an accusation.

She didn't know how to answer. He was watching her like she was some sort of unknown entity, certainly not like a woman who'd slept in his arms, who'd shared his life...

Don't go there, she told herself fiercely. Move on.

'My head's fine,' she told him. 'I'm fine.' Being dressed should make her feel better, more in control. It didn't. Somehow it made her feel defenceless.

The hurt she'd felt ten years ago was all around her. It was ridiculous, she told herself. You didn't mourn a lost love for ten years.

But the hurt had gone bone deep, and it was surfacing again now. This guy was too tall, his eyes were too dark. His hair was too black. He was too much the same as he'd been all those years ago.

'If you're running on a skeleton staff then I'm taking up a bed,' she managed. 'Discharge me now, Leo. The sooner I get out of this cell the happier I'll be.'

'Cell?'

'This room's awful. Why on earth don't you paint it?'

He didn't answer. The look on his face, though...

Uh-oh. She watched his fingers clench into fists at his sides, and then slowly unclench, as if he was counting to ten, and then to twenty, and then maybe to whatever it took to hold his temper.

'We have two private rooms in this entire hospital,' he said at last. 'We reserve them for those who desperately need privacy, usually those in the last days of their lives. We had a death just before you were admitted, which left this room free. Because of your...because of who you are... we believed a single room was imperative. Believe it or not, if we'd put you in a shared ward you would have had half the country visiting the patient in the next bed, just to get a look at you. So we did you a kindness. We put you in what's one of our best rooms.'

'Best rooms...'

'I told you, skeleton staff, minuscule budget, that's what we have. But certainly I'm happy for you to go. We started you on antibiotics last night. You can go as soon as the script's filled. Continue them for the full course—there are bats in those underground vaults and they carry infection. I can't imagine what Victoir was about, taking you down there without protective gear.'

'He was proving the place was unsafe.' There were a hundred other things she could have said but she couldn't get her tongue around any of them.

'It is unsafe. Obviously. But not if you know what you're doing.'

'You've been down there?'

'I'd imagine every adventurous child living within a couple of miles of the castle has been down there.'

'Bats or not?'

'They add to the challenge.'

'Surely my cousin didn't let kids into the castle.'

'There are entrances from outside the castle walls. No one's ever blocked them off. Your cousin and your uncle and your grandfather before him didn't give a toss what went on under the castle, as long as no one bothered their secluded, indolent lives. Let's get your head checked and get you out of here.'

'So I can start my secluded, indolent life?'

He sighed. 'Anna, I have no idea what you intend. I've heard Victoir plans to turn the castle into luxury apartments, with its own internal helipad. An oasis for the super-rich from other countries. With its location, with the Mediterranean right under the battlements, with the right design and your money behind it, such a place could be a celebrity magnet. He hired architects years ago, trying to persuade your cousin that it wouldn't intrude on his privacy. One of those architects left his plans in a local cab and the driver had them broadcast all over the country in minutes. It came to nothing, though. Your cousin wouldn't have seen anything in it for him, and that was all that interested him. Now, your head…'

'So he urgently wants the underground closed off because…'

'It wouldn't do to let it get out that the proposed idyllic retreat can be broached by twelve-year-olds.' He was right by her bed now, too close for comfort, but then anywhere in this tiny room was too close for comfort. 'Your head, Anna.

I'm here to examine you, not talk about plans that have nothing to do with me.'

That shut her up.

He checked her head, not disturbing the dressing over the gash but simply noting the extent of bruising. He checked her eyes, her vision, and then retreated to the end of the bed to read the obs chart. Time for discussion was over.

'Headache?' he asked as he finished reading.

'Only when I laugh, and when you're here I find it difficult to even smile.'

He didn't respond.

'Any dizziness?'

'When I stand up fast but that's to be expected.'

He nodded. 'Take it easy for a few days, then. Do what Victoir suggests. Go lie in your castle and enjoy your view.'

Oh, enough. She pushed herself to her feet and glared. 'That's mean. What have I ever done to you, Leo Aretino, to make you act like I'm something the cat dragged in?'

'That's an exaggeration.'

'It's not. What have I done?'

'You haven't done anything.'

'Once upon a time you asked me to marry you.'

'That was a long time ago.' He closed his

eyes—remembering?—and when he opened them there was a hint of softness there. Regret? 'We all do stupid things when we're young. Proposing to someone you barely know might count as one of them.'

'You did know me, though. You slept with me for—'

'I don't want to go there. It's history.'

'Which is affecting how you're treating me right now.'

'I'd be treating you the same if we hadn't slept together.'

'That's a lie and you know it. I watched you train as a doctor. I've seen you with patients. You're caring and kind, and last night you couldn't stop yourself moving in for a hug. Now I'm not going to be a patient any more, you're back to cold and sarcastic and all the things you suddenly became the moment you learned who my mother was.'

'Anna...'

'You owe it to me, Leo,' she said, calmly now. 'It's a question that's hung over me for years. I know I should have put it aside, but I've never understood. I suspect I'll be spending a bit of time here now, not only in your country but in this town. We may well meet again.' She took a deep breath, because what she was about to say was a concept so big she was having trouble getting her head around it. 'I may even be the one who decides on funding for this hospital.'

'Are you blackmailing me?' He was suddenly incredulous. 'What are you saying? Tell me why I didn't marry you or you'll cut off our funding?'

Whoa. It was her turn to be angry now.

She'd been confused about Leo for years. They'd had a glorious six months and then nothing. She'd felt hurt, betrayed, sick at heart, but he wouldn't talk of it. For what had remained of their training, he'd avoided any tutorial she was in. They'd been scrupulously polite when they'd been forced together.

She'd hurt every time she'd looked at him.

She'd been a kid, though, and those feelings should have long gone. She was now an experienced doctor in charge of her world—mostly—and there was no way she was letting this man insult her. Her anger was holding sway but she had herself in hand.

'Do you think I'd do that? Blackmail?' Her voice was so quiet that maybe only her dogs would have understood. It was the voice she used when she'd found them with a cornered, injured hedgehog.

Just before they'd decided never to annoy a hedgehog again.

'It's nothing to do with me, what you do,' Leo snapped.

'If I cut off your hospital funding, of course it's something to do with you.' She was having trouble getting the words out. 'You really think I would?'

'It's your right. Heaven knows, we've had to fight for what we have. You know you own this building? As landlord—'

'You think I'd close you down?'

'You're a Castlavaran.'

'So you think ruthlessness is genetic. It's like the name comes with a money-sucking piggy bank welded to my head.'

'I know the terms of your inheritance,' he said wearily. 'Of your Trust. You have no choice. Money goes into castle maintenance or your comfort. Our funding's limited to providing provisional medical care for Castlavarans and castle staff. We stretch that as far as we can, to provide for the rest of the island. The Trust's been in place for hundreds of years, written into the fabric of our constitution. You think we don't know that you can't break it?'

'I know I can't break it but I'm not about to change things. Your hospital is safe.'

'That's great. Thanks very much.'

'Stop the sarcasm.' She was getting very close to yelling. 'So I'm not threatening your hospital but there's still so much I don't understand. Ten years ago… Isn't it about time you told me why you wouldn't marry me?'

The junior nurse who'd helped her shower appeared at the door. Her eyebrows hit her hairline.

She disappeared, really, really fast.

Uh-oh.

Anna had spent enough time in hospitals to know what she'd just said would be all over the hospital—all over the country!—in minutes. Hospital grapevines were the same the world over.

Maybe she shouldn't have said it.

But, then, this guy had hurt her. Badly. For ten years she'd needed an explanation and right now she felt strong enough—and angry enough—to demand it.

'I told you why I couldn't marry you.' He raked his fingers through his dark hair, a gesture she remembered. A gesture she could almost feel. She knew what it was like to have those fingers…

Don't go there.

'You said there were family problems,' she threw at him. 'You said you could never marry a Castlavaran. You said if you did then you couldn't come home.'

'Which was the truth.'

'And I said if the feud's that bad then we could leave, go to Australia or Canada. I was ready to go anywhere with you, Leo. But you walked away.'

'I walked back here. To a country that needed me.'

'So you couldn't face family hostility. You chose your family over me.'

'I chose my country over you. I still do.'

'What, like I'm still available?'

'I never said that. I never meant—'

'I don't have a clue what you meant. You never explained. You just closed down.' She sighed. 'Enough. I'm over it or at least I should be. Falling in love with a toe-rag when I was a kid hasn't defined my life and it won't define me now. Neither will this inheritance. I have a lovely life back in England. I'll do what I need to do and go home and let you get on with it.'

'And let Victoir have his way.'

'He's head of the entire castle administration. You think I have any way of figuring out any better plan?'

'You could try.'

'And walk away from my life in England?' She shook her head and the dressing felt suddenly very heavy. 'Why would I do that? You were asked to change your life when you were nineteen and you made it clear that was impossible. Why should I even contemplate doing the same?'

So that went well.

Or not.

Leo left Anna's ward and stood in the corridor, staring at the plain, whitewashed wall in front of him.

Memories of ten years ago were all around him. Of Anna's white, shocked face as he'd told her he couldn't marry her. Of her reaction of total betrayal.

But how could he have done better? How could he have explained the contempt and hatred that was felt toward her family? As soon as he'd found out who she was, he'd felt his own dumb adolescent heart break. How to explain that his studies, his time in England, his hopes for his future and the trust his people had put in him, they'd all be destroyed if their relationship went further.

Ten years ago he'd faced a bleak choice. Marry Anna and take her back to Tovahna? Impossible. If her uncle accepted her as part of the family she—and he—would have been incorporated into a family he hated. The community who'd scraped to give him an education would have been betrayed.

And being honest, he had to accept there'd been another problem that had been bone deep. He and his mother had been dependent on charity since his father had died. To marry a Castlavaran and take her home, for her to be accepted as part of the Castlavaran family, and for him to be married to her... It'd be the story of Cinderella turned on its head, and at nineteen, sexist as it was, the idea had made him feel ill.

He'd tried to think of other options. Moving overseas, anywhere where two doctors could make a living without baggage? Cutting all ties to her family and to his island?

He couldn't do it. As soon as he'd heard her name he'd known he had to turn away.

So now... She was still angry? Maybe she had the right to be.

As he'd grown older he'd realised he should have explained better, but at nineteen, bewildered by the complexity of a love he'd been subsumed by, he'd hardly been able to get words out. To explain to his carefree, joyous Anna the abject poverty of his country, the hurt her family had inflicted on his... Explanations would have achieve nothing, he'd decided. It was better to walk away fast.

'Leo, I said you should charm the Castlavaran. I didn't say propose!' Carla's voice from the end of the corridor made him start. It was incredulous.

'What?'

'Luisa said she heard you talking about marriage!'

What the...? 'She was mistaken.' He turned to face her, willing his expression to be bland.

'She was sure.'

'We spoke in English. How's Luisa's English?'

'Poor,' she admitted. 'But she was adamant marriage was in the mix somewhere. She said you sounded intense. If not marriage… You weren't being accusatory, were you?'

'I wasn't.' He sighed and decided to be honest. 'We do have…baggage. Anna and I met at med school when I didn't know who she was. We were in the same class for six months. I haven't heard of her for years.'

'And you didn't tell us because…'

'Because, as I said, we have baggage,' he said, exasperated. 'We dated. Not for long, but what teenager spreads the word about his love life?'

'You had a love life with a Castlavaran?' Carla eyed him with incredulity. But then she winced.

Her wince had him distracted. He wanted to be distracted—he wanted *Carla* to be distracted—but not like this. 'Carla, your headache…'

'It's nothing.' She sounded annoyed with herself. 'It's almost gone.'

'Is there anything else wrong?'

'Apart from too many patients to see? So what's new?'

There was nothing new. The hospital normally had two fully trained doctors and two nurse-practitioners, nurses trained by Carla and Leo to take over many of their responsibilities. It was all they could manage when the cost of sending people abroad for medical training was prohibitive. But Bruno was on leave because his small son had fallen from a tree and fractured his leg. The little boy was currently undergoing corrective surgery in Italy. Freya was recovering from a filthy bout of the flu that had swept through the town, doubling their workload.

Carla had coped brilliantly during their absence, but for the first time ever Leo thought she looked...fragile?

'Carla, you look strained. Are you sure it's just a headache?'

'Truly, I'm better, but thanks for asking.' Their friendship went back a long way, and now she reached up and gave him a swift kiss on the cheek. 'There. A kiss better and I'm done. But a love affair with a Castlavaran? See me astonished. I demand that you take time later to tell me all about it. By the way, you're scratchy and I still think you should charm her. Teenage romances can be resurrected and if you want to charm our heiress you'd better go and shave.'

'I know where I'm going,' he growled. 'Off to check the morning list.'

'I didn't even look,' she told him. 'It's enough to terrify a woman stronger than me. But our heiress—your ex-girlfriend!—is a doctor? Maybe we could ask her to see a few coughs and colds before she goes back to her castle.'

'A Castlavaran? Treating peasants? In your dreams.'

'Don't be so cynical,' she told him. 'It isn't like you, and dreaming doesn't cost anything. I might just pop in and introduce myself.'

'You know there's no time.'

'There's no time for anything but medicine in this place,' Carla said, and suddenly she was deadly serious. 'But this woman holds our fate in her hands and she needs to be onside. I know what triage is, Dr Aretino, and triage says being nice to the Castlavaran is top of the list, for all our sakes. And you… I'm thinking a shave is the least of it.'

'Carla…'

'I know. I need to shut up and see the next patient, like I do all the time.'

The snap was so unlike her that he took her shoulders and forced her to meet his gaze. 'Carla? What is it? You're not coming down with the flu, are you?'

'Of course not,' she said defensively. 'It's just a headache.'

'How bad?'

'Nothing a good night's sleep won't fix. Or another doctor. This country…this health service… I try to be cheerful but sometimes it gets me down.'

'It gets us all down but we need to cope with what we have.'

'Or try and charm a Castlavaran,' she said grimly. 'I can but try, even if you won't. Off you go and start our list, Leo. I'll talk to the heiress and join you when I'm done.'

CHAPTER THREE

VICTOIR WAS BRINGING a car back from the castle. It'd be here in ten minutes, the nurse had told her. Anna was ready to go.

She practised sitting and standing a few times. No dizziness. Breakfast seemed to have settled her. Facing Leo should have settled her even more, and in a way it had.

For ten years she'd wondered what she'd say to him, and somehow she'd said it. It felt empty, desolate even, but it was done. It was time to head back to the castle and cope with the enormity of what lay before her. That was enough to make anyone dizzy.

She wasn't dizzy now, though. She was being realistic. What had been landed on her shoulders was far too much for one woman to take in.

Her life waited for her back in England—her dogs, her friends, her lovely little cottage. Her friends had been coaxing her to try a dating site. Maybe she could.

But relationships never seemed to work out for her. Her solitary childhood, her mother's constant abandonment and then Leo's bombshell rejection seemed to have left scars in the trust department. She dated men who were safe and steady, but then there was always that element of...boredom? Whatever it was, it seemed to stop things moving to the next level. She needed to get over it. It was time she dated someone who thought the world was fun.

And this? She didn't need to tell a prospective date about the enormity of her inheritance, she decided. There was nothing she could do about it for another twenty years. She'd hand it back to Victoir and set out to enjoy her uncomplicated life.

She'd have fun without the baggage her mother and then Leo had left her with.

'Can I come in?'

A woman peered around the door, short, rounded, her glasses perched low on her nose. She was wearing sturdy shoes and a white doctor's coat. A stethoscope dangled from her pocket, her white hair was bundled into a tousled bun and her face made Anna feel instinctively that here was someone she should welcome.

'Of course,' Anna told her. She was perched on the bed but stood up. Anna wasn't overly tall but the newcomer barely reached her shoulders.

'I'm Dr Rossini,' the woman said. 'Carla. I'm Leo's colleague.'

'It's good to meet you,' Anna said, and found her hand gripped in a hold that was strong and warm and strangely welcoming. It seemed a warmer welcome than she'd had from anyone in the three days she'd been in the country.

'I've brought you your antibiotics,' Carla said, handing over a box. 'I picked them up from the pharmacy. It'll save you fetching them as you go out. You understand you need to take the whole course?'

'I do. Thank you.'

'And I wanted to meet you,' Carla said. 'You should meet at least one member of the medical staff who doesn't think your name makes you poison.'

'Is that what everyone thinks?'

'Yes,' she said bluntly. 'With reason. If you want me to say nice things about your family you should ask me to go away. But I'm not judging you.'

'That's good of you,' she said wryly, and Carla gave her a rueful smile.

'Sorry. But I thought I should lay our cards on the table. Something I suspect Victoir won't do on our behalf. Maybe not even Leo.'

'Your cards?'

'The country's cards.'

'Right,' Anna said, and the ache in her head suddenly returned. Or maybe it was a different ache. It was the dull throb that had been there ever since she'd realised the enormity of her inheritance.

Strangely, Carla was putting her own hand to her head. Matching headaches? The last thing Anna wanted to do now was talk about the complexities she'd inherited, but she could see strain in the older woman's eyes. She suspected that what was about to be said would be hard to say.

'What's Leo told you about our country?' Carla asked.

'You know I know Leo?'

'He said you dated briefly, at med school. Did he explain the set-up here?'

Briefly? The word hung. It hurt. But she wouldn't talk about Leo. He didn't fit into this conversation—in any conversation she intended having.

Briefly...

'You know the Castlavarans own everything on this island,' Carla was saying. 'Everything. We're a tiny country. We should be centrally governed by a larger state but we've always been independent. Our own language. Our own resources. And, sadly, our own official family, a family that's scourged the land for its own ends and paid to subdue any unrest.'

'I understand that,' Anna said stiffly. 'I also understand there's little I can do about it for now. You know about the Trust? The terms of inheritance are that money from the estate is tightly held, used only for the upkeep of the castle or for my personal welfare. There's a twenty-year holding period before I can change that. Victoir says the Trust was put in place to prevent wild spending by past Castlavarans.

'I have trouble understanding the complexities, but legal opinion says I can't break it. It seems it's best if I go home, forget about it for twenty years and then put a team of lawyers in place to try and sort the mess out.' The ache in her head seemed to tighten. 'Even that boggles me.'

'I can imagine. But meanwhile you could try and help.'

'Like how?'

'Well, a steriliser for a start,' Carla said, suddenly sounding hopeful. And a little bit cheeky? She lifted a spoon from the cup and saucer, left from Anna's morning's coffee. 'This spoon, for instance. This is for your personal use and you're fussy. You could order a steriliser right now, to be delivered as soon as possible. We can't help it if you're discharged before you get to use it, and you could graciously allow us to use it until you need it again.'

Anna's lips twitched, and for the first time in what seemed weeks she found room to smile. In the enormity of what she'd been landed with, this seemed tiny, but the lovely thing about it was that it was something she could do right now.

Carla was looking hopeful, her head cocked to one side. Wondering if she was up to the challenge?

Maybe she was. *Fun.* The word was suddenly right before her. This was a baby step in how her life could continue from now on, but...could she have fun with this? Could she be of use?

'You know,' she said thoughtfully. 'These

sheets are scratchy. My welfare decrees I should order non-scratchy sheets, just in case I'm ever admitted again. Could you put in a requisition? Linen can't be kept apart in the hospital laundry so maybe enough for the whole hospital?'

'Yes!' Carla said, chuckling with delight. 'I knew you couldn't be as bad as your cousin. And what about coffee? You surely can't be expected to drink...' But then she paused. She put a hand to her head in a gesture Anna understood. Her own head hurt.

But this was suddenly more than that. Carla's pain seemed to intensify. Her eyes widened and she grabbed for the foot of the bed, as if to steady herself.

And swayed.

And Anna moved as she'd never moved before. She reached her and hugged her under her arms, taking her weight as she sagged against her.

As Carla's eyes became sightless. As her knees buckled.

As she crumpled to the floor.

Leo was in the nursery, checking the tiny baby who'd been born the night before. It was a good moment in what promised to be a frantic day. He gazed down at the newborn bundle and thought, This is what it's all about. Forget Anna. Forget the Castlavarans. Focus on what's important.

And then his buzzer...

Code blue.

He was out the nursery before he realised.

Room Twelve. *Anna's room.*

Code blue meant cardiac or respiratory arrest, or similar medical emergency.

Anna?

What had he missed? Internal bleed? What?

He didn't run—he didn't need to. He'd pretty much perfected his hospital stride, so running would make him no faster.

He turned the corner to Room Twelve and Maria was in front of him, pushing the crash cart.

'Anna...' he said, and he couldn't keep the fear from his voice.

'Worse,' Maria managed. 'It's Carla.'

She'd hit the call button and then she'd yelled. The junior nurse who'd helped shower her had arrived in seconds, taken one look and bolted for help.

Carla vomited as she reached the floor. The

first couple of moments were frantic, clearing Carla's airway, getting her into the recovery position, trying to assess her breathing. Anna was crouched on the floor, willing help to arrive. Trying to see what she was coping with. Cardiac arrest? No? Headache, pain, collapse...

And then blessedly Leo was kneeling beside her. The crash cart was being wheeled in behind him.

'Carla...' Leo said, and she heard his voice break.

Carla's eyes were open but she wasn't seeing.

'I don't think it's her heart.' Anna said it intentionally loudly, making her voice clipped and professional. Leo and this woman must be friends. She'd heard Leo's instinctive distress, but she needed a doctor here, not someone emotionally involved.

And he got it. She felt the moment he hauled himself together. The moment he became one of a medical team.

'Fall?'

'Collapse,' she told him. She glanced up at Maria, and Maria anticipated her needs by handing down a towel. Two. She used one to sweep the mess away from Carla's head, the other to help clear her face. 'She looked like her head hurt. She put her hand to her head like there was intense pain and then she passed out.'

'The headache... Hell...' He had his hand on her wrist.

'It's still strong,' Anna told him.

They were squashed together. Maria started working around them, shoving the bed back, heaving the bedside table onto the bed to give them more room.

'Defibrillator?' Maria asked.

'No.' Leo was moving to the next stage. He checked her eyes, and Anna saw the slight sag of his shoulders, relief that he'd seen a corneal reflex. He'd seen her clear Carla's mouth. He'd seen the gag reflex as well.

She wasn't comatose, then, but the speed of the drop from alert to where she was now implied she soon would be.

'It's okay, Carla, we've got you,' Leo said, loudly and firmly. 'Relax, love, don't fight it.'

That made Anna blink. He was assuming Carla could hear. It was good medicine, the assumption, unlikely as it was, that Carla would comprehend what was going on. But not all doctors did it, especially under the stress of an emergency like this one.

'We need to stabilise your airway and get a scan,' Leo said. 'Carla, have you had a head injury? Banged your head?' She didn't respond—how could she?—but once again Anna knew the words had been said to reassure Carla that she was included in this conversation. 'Carla didn't say anything about an injury, Anna? Maria?'

'Nothing,' Maria said, and Anna heard her distress, too.

'Just a headache,' Anna said. 'Leo, this looks like an internal bleed.'

'You must have had a bump.' Leo was back to speaking to Carla. 'You told me you took aspirin last night.'

'She has been taking aspirin,' Maria ventured. 'She's been getting it from the hospital pharmacy. I saw her take a couple of boxes last week. She said she has a bit of arthritis. We were busy and I didn't follow it up.'

'Aspirin won't have done this, though it might have made it worse,' Leo said. 'But if there's a bleed it won't help now. Carla, we're going to have to have a look-see. Get a trolley, Maria. We'll take her through for scans. Now.'

'What can I do?' Anna asked.

'You're a patient,' Leo said roughly. 'Thanks for your help, Anna. You should be right to go.'

The scan showed a bleed.

A big one.

The hairline skull fracture was bad enough. What was worse was the dark shadow underneath the fracture. A subdural haemorrhage. Blood vessels near the surface of the brain had obviously ruptured.

How the hell...?

But the cause of the injury was the least of his concerns. What was crucial was time. Blood had collected immediately beneath the three-layer protective covering of the brain. The brain was being compressed.

In young people a bleed like this was usually triggered by a significant impact. Older people could bleed after only a minor trauma.

Carla was hardly elderly but she'd been taking aspirin. The aspirin would have been thinning the blood.

The greater the pressure on the brain, the worse the bleeding would become. For her to lose consciousness so quickly...

'I'm going in.' He was talking to Carla, and to the nurse beside him. Maria was looking as terrified as he felt. 'Carla, there's a bleed under the surface. We need to get the pressure off.' He needed to say no more. If Carla was aware enough to take it in then she'd know, and Maria had been a nurse long enough to realise the ramifications of a cranial bleed. Pressure on the brain caused brain damage, and it caused it fast. They had to get the pressure off now.

'Leo, I'm asking again. What can I do?'

The voice came from the doorway. Anna still looked very much the patient. She was dressed in jeans and a T-shirt, but the white dressing showed starkly against her burnt-red hair.

'You need to leave, Anna.' It was an instinctive response.

'I'm a doctor, Leo,' she snapped. 'Get over yourself. Let me help.'

'You're injured.'

'I have stitches from a bump on my head. I imagine Carla's haemorrhaging. Am I right?'

'You're not well. I can't—'

'Do you have another doctor on staff? An anaesthetist?'

He needed headspace and she was messing

with it. He opened his mouth to snap back but sense prevailed.

His instinctive reaction to Anna had been that of a doctor to a patient. The internal war, how he was feeling about Carla's illness, physician versus friend, could allow no other distractions.

Anna's question, though, had cut through.

There was no other doctor within hours of travel. Carla collapsing so dramatically meant that the bleed was sudden and severe. The pool of blood under the dura must be causing damage.

Carla usually assumed the role of anaesthetist if he needed to operate. What now?

'There's no other doctor,' he admitted.

'Evacuation?'

'It'll take hours.'

'Then she needs emergency craniotomy and drainage,' Anna said. Her curt, professional tone helped. 'If there's no one else... Leo, can you operate if I do the anaesthetic? I've done additional anaesthetic training. The village where I work isn't big enough to support medical specialists and there's occasional urgent need.'

She had anaesthetic training? It was like a gift from the heavens. A colleague with anaesthetic skills...

'You have a head injury yourself.'

'I have stitches and bruising. I may also still suffer a bit of dizziness if I stand up fast, but I think I'm over it and I can cover it. I know it's not ideal but given the circumstances… Give me a stool in Theatre and let's move.'

He gazed down at Carla and saw no response. No glimmer of recognition. He looked again at Anna and she met his gaze with a determination that was almost steely. Treat me as a doctor, her gaze said. Get over your prejudices.

She was still a patient. He could hardly ask.

There was no choice.

'Thank you,' he said simply. 'If you're sure.'

'I'm sure. Let's move.'

The surgery sounded simple. Anyone with a decent handyman's drill should be able to do it—in fact, Leo had heard of doctors in emergency situations using just such an implement.

Luckily he didn't have to resort to such measures. Most of their of equipment was second-hand but it was functional. Leo had kept up with a lot of doctors he'd met during training, and when they had been purchasing shiny new medical toys they often remembered him and sent on usable older things. The X-ray department had been set up almost completely via donations from a friend he'd met in final year med school. For the rest they'd scraped and saved and cajoled the community, which meant the theatre he was working in was fully equipped.

And he had excellent staff. Maria, his chief nurse, was rigid about standards and ongoing training, and she ruled her nursing staff with a softly gloved fist of iron.

The only hole in the team was his lack of a trained anaesthetist and that hole had been plugged. In Anna he had an anaesthetist he could trust. From the moment he'd nodded his acceptance of her offer she'd turned almost instantly from patient, from heir to the powers of Castlavara, from his past lover—into a crisp, competent professional.

'Do you have access to Carla's medical history? I need to know what she's taken, allergies… Family? Is someone on their way?'

'Her husband died ten years back,' he told her. 'Her son's in Italy. But we have her history. Maria…'

'Onto it,' Maria said, and so was Anna. Ten minutes later they were in Theatre.

'Glasgow scale deteriorating,' Anna told him. 'I'm losing any eye response.'

He didn't need telling. He knew the pressure would be building.

He needed to focus.

A handyman might be able to operate a drill but what was needed here was precision, care, knowledge. And confidence.

Confidence that Anna could keep Carla alive while he worked.

And strangely the trust was there.

If another doctor had walked in right now, someone he didn't know... If they'd offered to help... Yes, he'd have had to accept their help but there'd be caution. He'd be checking all the time. He'd be torn, though, because the procedure he was performing was out of his comfort zone. He needed to work fast with skills he hardly knew he had.

Anna helped. Somehow just knowing she was here helped.

Carla was in the supine position, facing up. As soon as Anna had the IV line in, as soon as she was sure Carla was under, Maria did a quick shave.

Then it was over to Leo. Two small holes to expose the dura, then careful, painstakingly draining. Hell! The scan had showed a build-up but it shook him to see just how much fluid was in there.

He inserted a temporary drain to prevent more build-up. He'd rather not have—it increased the chance of infection—but with this amount of fluid and with the speed of onset of symptoms, he had little choice.

Then closing.

It sounded straightforward. It seemed the hardest surgery he'd ever undertaken. Why? Because the huge unknown was how much damage had already been done. Had they been fast enough? Had the pressure already caused irreparable harm?

He fixed the drainage tube, dressed the wound and finally stood back from the table.

He'd done all he could do.

Carla was his friend and he felt ill.

What would have happened if Anna hadn't been here? Would he have had to administer the anaesthetic himself? Have Maria do it?

Or wait for evacuation?

He was under no illusion as to what waiting would have meant. Even now, as Anna reversed the anaesthetic, he was aware that they might have been too late. Cerebral haemorrhage was the most frightening of medical emergencies.

'We've done everything we can,' he said wearily. 'A neurosurgeon will need to take over. We've put in a call for evacuation but that's still hours away. Meanwhile, we just have to hope.'

Anna had finished reversing the anaesthetic. She'd removed the intubation tube. Carla was breathing for herself again, but would she wake up? And if she did, what damage had been done?

'You went in as fast as you could,' she said, maybe sensing just how close to the edge he was. 'She has the best chance you could possibly have given her.'

'Partly thanks to you.' Then, almost huskily, 'Thank you.'

'Don't thank me.'

He nodded, dumbly, as the imperatives of surgery faded and the fear for his friend flooded back. What if the damage from pressure was irreversible? What if Carla didn't open her eyes again, or, if she did, what life would she be facing?

Surely they'd moved fast enough.

With this level of bleeding, with the speed with

which things had overtaken Carla, there was no way of knowing.

There was nothing more he could do but wait. The pain he was feeling was fathoms deep.

'The Italian neurosurgeons will take over,' he said roughly. 'We don't have the facilities to do more.' While there'd been medical need, he'd been able to put distress aside, but now there was little to do for Carla but wait, that distress was impossible to hide. 'I need to speak to her son. Our receptionist will have contacted him already and he may well be on his way. But enough. Anna, you need to go home.'

'Leaving you alone.'

'Bruno will be back later today. He's one of our nurse-practitioners but his six-year-old fell out of a tree last week. Comminuted fracture of his femur. He needed specialist orthopaedic care.'

'So he was evacuated, too?'

'Yes, but Bruno should be back.'

'But he's not a doctor.'

'He's good. Anna, you need to leave. I'll take over here.'

'And leave you to worry about Glasgow scores on your own.'

'You're a patient, Anna,' he said, reminding himself as well as her. 'Your place isn't here.'

He saw her wince, but there was nothing he could do about it. He had room for nothing but distress for his friend.

And she seemed to accept it. She looked at him for a long moment and then nodded.

'Okay. But you will call me if Carla needs me. If *you* need me.'

'I will.' He hesitated. 'But the castle won't necessarily put my calls through.'

'What the…? Of course they will.'

'Try and see,' he said wearily. 'The outside world isn't permitted to intrude on the castle and its occupants.'

'That might have been then,' she said briskly. 'This is now. If there's any problem, I have my own phone and it's on international roaming. I'll leave my number at the desk. Call me. Promise?'

And he looked at her, a long look where questions were being asked that he didn't understand and maybe she couldn't respond to.

'I promise,' he said at last. 'Not that I think it'll happen, but I promise. Thank you, Anna, but you need to remember you've been injured yourself. It's time for you to leave.'

CHAPTER FOUR

To say Victoir was annoyed was an understatement. He'd come to collect her in one of the castle's limousines. He'd been left kicking his heels for hours.

When she finally joined him he was leaning on the beautiful auto, glowering, looking almost startlingly out of place. The entrance to the hospital was serviceable but that was all that could be said about it. It was a narrow driveway, crammed with people coming and going, mothers and babies, the elderly in wheelchairs or Zimmer frames, people visiting with bunches of flowers or bags of washing.

The ambulance that had transported Anna to hospital the day before had backed into the entrance parking bay, in front of the limo. The limo was practically taking up the entire bay. Paramedics were trying to manoeuvre an elderly lady on a stretcher around Victoir. Victoir, in his immaculate dark suit and crisp white linen, with his hair sleeked back, a man in his forties in charge of his world, wasn't about to move for anyone, not even a patient on a stretcher.

The sight made Anna wince. Not for the first time she thought helplessly about the terms of the castle Trust. Yes, she'd inherited but she had no power. Once upon a time one of her ancestors had mistrusted his heir and made the entailment bulletproof. It would be twenty years before she had any control over funds. She owned it all and yet she didn't own it.

Her cousin hadn't survived his inheritance for the twenty years needed to break the Trust. Her uncle and her grandfather…clearly by the time their twenty years had been up they hadn't bothered. After all, why should they? All their needs were being met.

Men like Victoir had no doubt been lining their own pockets, but to find out how, to explore the complexities of things she probably could do nothing about…

'Leave it and come home,' Martin had suggested. 'A decent legal team can look after your interests from over here. If in twenty years you wish to do something more, you can think about options then.'

It made sense. She knew little about this place except that she now—sort of—owned it. And it was poverty-stricken. And Leo was here and he was struggling.

Victoir was opening the car door for her. 'You should have asked the nurses to carry your gear. That's what they're here for.'

Really? It was a small holdall. To ask one of the overworked medical staff to abandon their work to carry it…

'I can't believe they let you just walk out with it,' he continued. 'If they think they can treat a Castlavaran like—'

'They treated me well.'

'They asked you to work! When you're ill yourself?'

'I'm not ill and I asked to work.'

'They've even demanded to come to the castle. A final check, the nurse said. As if we can't take care of you.'

An offer of a follow-up visit by a district nurse was entirely reasonable, Anna thought. She'd have organised the same for a patient of hers. She didn't need it, though. She was okay.

Except that she was angry.

Usually she was unflappable. She prided herself on her calm in the face of crises.

She didn't feel calm now.

Get a grip, she told herself. Think of the whole situation.

Until now she'd floundered, bowing to Victoir's assumed authority. What choice had she had? But his authority was starting to grate and grate badly. Surely she paid this man's wages?

She didn't know how much. By the look of his clothing and the gold rings on his flaccid fingers, a lot. She'd spent her short time here trying to come to terms with the vastness of her inheritance. Should she stay a few more days and check staff ledgers? She could do that as she lay on her day bed while the staff in question catered to her every whim, she thought, and then she grimaced. The only appealing part of that right now was the day bed.

'You need to remember you've been injured yourself.'

That was what Leo had said and there had been gentleness in his tone.

Of course there had. She was his patient. His gentleness meant nothing.

She'd been judged ten years ago and he'd

walked away. How much deeper would that judgement be now that she'd inherited?

'Can you get that ambulance out of the way?' Victoir called, power loading every word. And to Anna's disgust, the paramedic left the old lady's trolley where it was, and went to move the ambulance.

'You'll look after your patient first,' she called, and Victoir's authority was nothing compared to the power she put behind her words. Wow. Where had that come from? Was it the doctor in Anna, or was it the first stirrings of the long line of autocratic Castlavarans in her genetics? Regardless, her words held the weight of ancestry, plus a huge loading of a doctor accustomed to sorting chaos in the midst of medical emergency. It forced all those around her to go still.

The paramedic, the woman about to climb back into the driver's seat, looked at her with doubt. Anna might sound authoritative but she surely couldn't look it. Jeans, T-shirt, bandaged head. What remained of her copper curls tumbling every which way. No make-up. Compared to Victoir she looked a nothing.

But this was a test she needed to pass. Victoir was looking at her as if she'd passed the bound-

aries of what was permitted. Up until now he'd
set the guidelines. He'd made it easy for her to
follow his lead, impossible for her to do anything else.

Impossible had to start somewhere. Victoir was
invoking the family name? So could she.

'I'm Anna Castlavara and we wait until the
needs of patients have been met,' she said. 'Your
patient's care takes precedence over my needs.'

'We've waited long enough,' Victoir snapped.
'These people—'

'These people are Tovahnans, just like me,' she
said. 'What's best for them is best for me. And
what I say goes.'

And she seated herself—firmly—in the rear
of the limousine and prepared to wait.

But what she hoped Victoir didn't see was that
she sat not because she needed to but because
her knees were shaking.

What was she letting herself in for?

And then she glanced out of the window of the
car and there was Leo. He was striding out to
check on the new patient being admitted.

He'd paused like everyone else.

He'd heard.

So what? She turned away, putting her hands

to her cheeks to try and subdue the slow burn spreading across her cheeks. Her knees were still trembling.

She needed that day bed.

She needed space.

She needed to get home to England.

The evacuation team was delayed and delayed again. It happened. Neighbouring countries assisted as they could, but their own emergencies took precedence over Tovahna's. Finally, though, and before evacuation took place, Carla regained consciousness.

It was six at night. She'd been unconscious for almost ten hours. She was confused, her speech was a little blurred and she wasn't sure what was happening or why, but she recognised Leo. She recognised Maria. Her vision seemed only slightly impaired. Her fingers and toes worked, albeit with a struggle.

'What...what...? Tell me what's happened.'

The spectre of unimaginable brain damage faded. It was so much more than Leo had dared hope that it was all he could do to hold back tears.

Maria couldn't. She sobbed, openly. 'Oh, Carla,

we've been so frightened. You nearly died. And the Castlavaran, Anna, had to help save you.'

'The Castlavaran…' Carla managed. 'What…? Tell me…'

So Leo sat beside her and held her hand and told her. He wasn't sure if she took it all in. You didn't suffer a bleed on the brain without some repercussions, he thought, but her state of awareness now was a huge promise of a short rehabilitation and total recovery.

'Do you remember banging your head?' he asked, and she looked blank.

'The Castlavaran, Anna, banged her head.'

She was remembering. Better and better.

'She did.'

'And you're dating her.'

Hell. 'I'm not.'

'I remember—'

'Carla…'

'That would be so wonderful.'

And there was no response to that. Carla's eyes were closing. With the amount of drugs on board, the battering her brain had taken, her body was demanding sleep.

But it was sleep, not lack of consciousness. What a gift.

'Thanks to Anna,' Maria whispered. 'We need to let her know.'

'I'll see to it,' he said, and he left Maria watching Carla like a mother hen with her favourite chick.

We need to let her know...

He had Anna's number. He should simply ask the receptionist to ring a message through.

But before he could do anything he was hailed from down the corridor by two young men. One was Ben, Carla's son, who he guessed had hitched a ride in with the evacuation team from Italy. The other was Bruno, the nurse-practitioner. The evacuation team was behind them, signing in at Reception.

He hadn't realised how tired he was until he saw them. An almost-doctor to share his load. A son to take over his love for Carla and to accompany her on evacuation. Trained paramedics to take Carla to a world-class neurologist.

'You look like a car crash.' Bruno's voice was filled with concern. 'I came as soon as I could. And here's Ben to be with his mother. Tell us the worst, Leo.'

But it wasn't the worst. He felt himself growing even lighter.

'There's every reason to think she'll make a full recovery,' he told them. 'She'll need full neurological assessment but now…the real concern is how she came to have the bleed in the first place.'

'I can tell you that,' Ben said grimly. 'When I rang her last night she said she'd had a headache, then hit her head on the open bathroom cabinet and made it worse. She was making light of it but I could tell she was rattled.'

'But she still came to work this morning.' Hell. They were so short-staffed. Carla would have come to work with more than a sore head.

He might have done the same.

'I'll be having words with her,' Ben growled. 'I know she's popping aspirin for her arthritis. Once she's evacuated to Italy I'll insist on some enforced R&R, and have her visit an arthritis specialist while she's there.' He coloured. 'I have the money to afford it.'

'There's no need to sound apologetic,' Bruno said. 'I just took my son to Italy to have a complex fracture seen to. We each look after our own as best we can.' He glanced up at Leo. 'I hear we even treat Castlavarans.'

'She's not that bad,' Leo said grudgingly. 'You

know she's a doctor? She gave the anaesthetic while I operated on Carla.'

'She did what?' To say they were both astounded was an understatement.

'She did all she could.' He told them briefly what had happened. 'She's a talented doctor.'

'Well, pigs might fly,' Bruno said, and whistled. 'All this while she had her own sore head.'

'I need to thank her,' Ben said. 'She's still here?'

'She's back in the castle.'

'Well, that's that, then,' Bruno concluded. 'The castle walls have been broached and sealed again.'

'We don't know that,' Leo told him.

'Really? Does she intend to help anyone else in this country? Like repair the roof on this dump?'

'You know the Trust stops her.'

'Then I'm not interested,' Bruno said. 'It was good of her to help Carla but it's over to us again. Tell Ben where his mother is. Give me a handover, sign off with the evac team and then go home for a sleep.'

Sleep. The word was like a siren song, infinitely enticing.

But he did need to ring Anna. She deserved to know how Carla was.

'Go on,' Bruno growled. 'Out of my hospital. Now.'

'Your hospital?'

'Okay, it's the Castlavarans',' Bruno admitted. 'But there's nothing we can do about that. We just have to make do with the scraps they leave us.'

He wasn't wanted.

Well, he was. There was work for him to do, but Bruno was having none of it. 'You're no use to us dead on your feet. You know if there's a need I'll call you back.'

Bruno was right. He did need to sleep, but how could he head home and sleep after a day like today? He felt wired. Disoriented.

Seeing Anna had done that to him.

He'd promised to let her know.

He went to collect her phone number from Reception but then hesitated.

Anna was less than half a mile away, within the walls of the great castle that dominated the whole island.

She was with Victoir and his precious, urgent

documents. Heaven knew what he'd have her sign. Would she even think about what consequences her signature could have over so much of the island?

He glanced out toward the castle walls, vast and imposing. Victoir wanted to turn the castle into apartments for the wealthy, but everyone knew the terms of Anna's inheritance. Funds could only be used for her welfare or the upkeep of the castle. Luxury apartments... How could Victoir get away with that under the terms of the Trust? But if he could... Would Anna realise how much it would hurt the islanders?

Despite its generations of miserly owners, the castle still seemed the beating heart of Tovahna. For hundreds of years Tovahnans had lived within the shadow of its walls. Their forebears—Leo's forebears—had fought for it.

He'd seen Victoir's plans. What they proposed was tearing down sections of the wall to insert massive plate-glass windows, so those lucky enough to afford to stay here could see the islanders going about their business. Victoir knew his market. He wanted the world's rich and famous to use this as a retreat, and quaint island life—at a distance—was a marketing tool.

Did Anna know that poverty was one thing, rubbing the islanders' noses in the riches of others was another?

He thought of Victoir's face as Leo had agreed with Anna's assertion that she was unfit to sign. He'd have the documents out again already, he thought. She might have already signed.

She was his patient. More, she was his colleague and she'd helped save his friend. He needed to see her.

'It's the least I can do,' he muttered to himself.

And then he turned toward the castle.

He took the sea walk to the castle entrance. The walk itself did him good. It was early evening and the harbour was alive with fishing boats unloading, families coming down to help sort the catch, kids playing between lobster pots, cheerful banter between rival fishermen.

It was an idyllic setting. It disguised the grinding poverty underneath.

The idyll paled as he reached the castle walls. The massive stone fortress cast long shadows, and by the time he reached the vast oak and iron gates he felt cold.

Apartments. According to the Trust they'd have to be for Anna's private pleasure. She was a doctor and a good one. He'd seen her immediate concern for Carla. How could Victoir's grandiose plan ever give her pleasure?

And with that came another thought, maybe just as crazy. If medicine itself gave her pleasure then...then...

Don't, he told himself. You're here to protect her, make sure she's healing. Don't think past that.

First, face Victoir.

Islanders worked here—of course they did. They used the tradesmen's entrance, though, but tonight Leo was damned if he'd use the tradesmen's entrance.

He rang the bell and heard its sonorous tone echo behind the great stone walls. Few people rang this bell, he thought. Few people were welcome.

As he'd suspected, it was Victoir who answered the intercom. Victoir who controlled all intercourse between the castle and the world beyond. He'd been Yanni's private secretary, but under Yanni's indolent, indifferent rule his role had gone well past that.

'Dr Aretino...' Leo glanced up and saw cameras above his head. Of course. The castle's massive moat was no longer used for defence, but defences were still there.

'Victoir,' he said, struggling to keep irritation from his voice. 'I'm here to see Dr Raymond.'

'She's resting.' His tone was curt, dismissive.

'That's why I'm here. She suffered concussion. She needs to be checked. I gather you refused the offer of our district nurse when you left the hospital. She needs at least one more check within the forty-eight-hour period after injury.

'I can do that.'

The thought of Victoir checking made his skin crawl. It was all he could do to keep his voice even.

'You'll tell Dr Raymond I'm here to assess her medically and to give her an update on Dr Carla's condition,' he managed. 'I need to hear from her personally.'

'You're not welcome.'

He should turn around and leave.

He didn't.

'You have my patient in there,' he said, each word ringing loudly in the warm dusk. 'I'm concerned about her head injury. I need to be assured that she's well.'

'You can take my word for it.'

'That's not enough. Unless you can produce a medical power of authority, I need to either speak to Dr Raymond myself or I'll ask the local justice to demand access. You know I can do that, Victoir.'

The island justice would like nothing better than an excuse to demand entry to the castle and Victoir knew it. Leo heard the hesitation, the doubt, the weighing up of options.

Having the local authorities demanding entry would not suit Victoir's sense of control.

'She's asleep,' he said, and he sounded almost sulky.

'Do you know how to differentiate between deep sleep and unconsciousness?'

Another pause. And then a heavy click and the vast gates started opening.

'A quick check and you're out of here,' Victoir growled, but Leo didn't bother to answer.

She wasn't asleep. She'd tried hard enough. Home from the hospital, she'd felt weariness envelop her like a dead weight. It was reaction, she'd thought. She'd headed for bed in her over-the-top bedroom but she hadn't slept.

Victoir had opened the door and checked on

her—twice—and that had freaked her out. The man gave her the creeps. She wanted to shove a chair against the door to make her secure but that'd show him he made her nervous. For some reason she didn't want him to see that.

She was wearing her yoga gear rather than her pyjamas because that made her feel safer—but not much. She'd feigned sleep and he'd gone away.

This whole place was weird, this over-the-top castle, its living quarters a monument to excess, the rest a derelict shambles. Given other circumstances the gothic setting could have entranced her, but now, alone, her head aching, what was on the other side of her bedroom door made her shudder.

She'd thought fleetingly of ringing Martin or Jennifer. If she said she was in trouble she knew they'd be on the next plane. They were good friends and they were sensible. They'd pick her up and bundle her home.

That was what she wanted right now, her friends, her dog, her own bed in her own small cottage. And yet… Somehow the events of the last twenty-four hours had made her feel that leaving was cowardly.

But right now cowardly seemed a good way to

describe her. This room seemed almost designed to make her feel insignificant, with its massive size, its vast crimson and gold wall hangings, its casement windows looking almost all the way to Italy.

There was a knock at the door and she clenched her teeth so hard she thought she might break them. At least this time he'd had the decency to knock.

'Yes?'

'Anna.'

It wasn't Victoir. *Leo.*

Surely she shouldn't feel relief, but she did. The tension evaporated in such a rush that she couldn't respond. She lay absolutely still.

'Anna?' She must be lying too still, too rigid. There was deep concern in his voice.

Leo…concerned for her…

It made her feel like her world was settling.

She was being dumb, she thought. It was this castle that was unnerving her, this creepy gothic setting, these vast, opulent living areas, this huge bedchamber.

But Leo was here. 'Come in,' she called, and finally she allowed herself to open her eyes and look.

Leo.

Not professional Leo either. He'd ditched the white coat. He was wearing faded jeans and a cotton shirt with the sleeves rolled to the elbows and the top buttons undone. His hair was tousled, as if he'd been walking in the wind.

Once upon a time she'd thought…she'd dreamed…

No.

'Hey,' she said, and summoned a smile—and saw relief wash his face.

He'd been worried. Despite her confusion the thought was comforting.

'You're okay?' he asked, the crease deepening between his eyes. Oh, those eyes…

'Nothing a good sleep won't fix.' She gazed up at him and saw her own weariness reflected. 'Same for you, I bet. What are you doing here?'

'Checking up on you. Victoir knocked back the offer of a district nurse.'

'I don't need the district nurse.' She sat up and wrapped her arms around her knees. 'How can I need anything in this room?'

'I guess you don't,' he admitted. He gazed around the bedroom. 'Great setting.'

'It's ridiculous,' she muttered, and decided she

needed to be a bit assertive. She needed to sound as if she was in charge of her world again.

'Really ridiculous,' she emphasised. 'Not just one but two—*two!*—chandeliers. For a bedroom. Ten guest chairs. Two settees and a window seat big enough to seat me, my dogs and a small army of minions—if I wanted minions, which, believe me, I don't. And this carpet... Who chooses crimson and purple carpet with dragons woven into it? And it's not even the main bedroom—I gather this was one of Yanni's guest rooms. *Urk.*'

'I guess you could learn to like it,' he said neutrally, but there was a faint smile behind his eyes. He agreed with her, then. 'Anna, now I'm here... Headache? Pain level? One to ten, you know the score.'

'Two,' she admitted. 'Nothing an aspirin won't fix.'

'Let's try paracetamol instead,' he told her. 'I gather aspirin is what was behind Carla's bleed. She's been taking it for arthritis and then bumped her head. On the medicine cabinet, her son says.'

'Ouch.' They both knew aspirin could make a small bleed worse. 'But now...' She couldn't keep anxiety from her voice.

'She's awake and alert. She's a bit confused but

she knows people, events, and there's no notice-
able physical damage. Her son's with her. She's
on her way to a full neurological assessment in
Italy but she may well be in the clear.'

'Oh, Leo, that's wonderful.'

'It is, isn't it?' he said, and smiled and pulled
up one of her overstuffed visitor chairs to sit beside her.

Which was discombobulating all on its own.

Leo. Beside her.

Get over it.

'Where's Victoir?' she managed.

'Do you care?'

'He's my...' She hesitated. 'Actually, I don't
know what he is. The boss of me? That's what
he'd like to think. I'm a bit over Victoir.'

'Good for you. Are you going to sign the release so he can build his apartments?'

She stilled.

She hadn't gone completely to bed. She'd put
her head on the mound of glorious pillows and
tucked the great crimson coverlet over her. Her
yoga gear was pink and purple and covered her
nicely.

She wanted more.

She wanted to be in crisp, professional work

clothes. She didn't want to be in a room lit by chandeliers and carpeted with dragons. Most of all, she wanted some sort of protection against this crazy situation, where on one hand she'd inherited power and on the other hand she had no power at all.

'What's that got to do with you?' she asked, and then thought, I sound petty. He must have thought so, too, as his face hardened.

'Everything. You turn this castle into apartments, you rip the heart out of my people.'

'Why does that sound like the overstatement of the year?'

'I'm not exaggerating. The castle takes up almost a quarter of the island. Your grandfather, your uncle and your cousin were appalling rulers but the islanders have accustomed themselves to this life for generations. The people should have risen up long ago but they haven't. They won't. And now… Turn the castle into a glorified gated community where the super-rich can fly in and fly out… Maybe there will be an uprising. I almost hope so, but it'll take years, and meanwhile there's nothing here. There's no hope for the kids. This island needs help, Anna, and right now the only help available is from you.'

'So how could I possibly help?'

'By not being a Castlavaran.'

'Don't you get that I'm not?' Enough. She shoved the coverlet back, folded her arms across her chest and glared.

His reaction wasn't quite what she'd hoped. He looked totally distracted. 'Great outfit,' he said faintly, and the smile returned to his eyes.

'I like pink.' She folded her arms across her chest and glowered. 'And purple.'

'Why wouldn't you? It's amazing.'

'Leo, the last thing I want is compliments,' she snapped, and stood up.

Or tried to. The effects of the last twenty-four hours were still with her. She swayed.

Leo rose and caught her as she staggered. He lowered her gently so she was sitting on the side of the bed.

She should be thankful.

She wasn't.

'I just stood up too fast,' she muttered.

'I know. Anger makes us do all sorts of unwise things.'

'What's that supposed to mean?' She had herself together again—a bit. Oh, she wished she wasn't wearing pink and purple. More than that, she wished she was somewhere neutral, not in this ridiculous bedroom, and not feeling so defenceless. And, yes, angry.

'Don't mouth platitudes at me, Leo Aretino,' she managed, anger growing. 'For ten years you assumed I knew what you were talking about. That I was part of this system. You assumed my cousin's, my uncle's, my grandfather's greed was not only known to me but that their actions were somehow partly my fault. It's not my fault, Leo. So now... I'm not a Castlavaran but I'm stuck.

'The terms of this inheritance are unequivocal. The money's to be used for the castle's upkeep. For my upkeep. Victoir's plan is that he build the apartments, and nominally I holiday in one. The rest are for my so-called friends to join me. We can defend it by saying it's "for my pleasure". It's a way we can close off the unsafe sections and keep the rest of the place functional, even economically viable, while I get on with my life. How else can I stop the whole place from falling down? The way Victoir presents it, I don't see that I have much choice.'

'You can look at options.'

'As if I'd know what they are. So if you have

any, tell me, Leo, and stop treating me as the enemy.'

'I never—'

'You did,' she managed. She was so mad she was trembling. Was that still the residue from the bump on the head? Or residue from being dumped ten years ago. Who knew? Not her. 'From the moment my mother told you her maiden name, you've treated me like some form of alien, more, one capable of contaminating anyone who came near. So now… I accept this is your country and your concern. You don't like Victoir's option? Give me another.'

Her anger was almost a tangible thing. There was so much past history here, betrayal, hurt— and a love that had once consumed her.

Get over it, she told herself. Listen.

Without prejudice.

'There is a way,' Leo said, his calm voice trying to break through her obvious fury. 'Anna, can you listen? I'm not sure, but there might be.'

What was he about to say? Break the Trust? Martin had said it was inviolable.

'Like what?' Her anger was still obvious but she couldn't help it.

'Using Victoir's idea,' he said, and she blinked.

'The apartments.'

'No.' He closed his eyes for a moment, and took a couple of breaths. Calm or not, he sounded as if was holding himself in rigid control. Maybe the tension she was feeling between them wasn't one-sided?

If so, good, she thought, and then had the grace to feel ashamed. Yes, he'd dumped her but she'd gone on to have a pretty good life. Maybe her anger was out of proportion. But still, he'd hurt her. She wanted him to acknowledge that.

But he was now intent on his plan. Focussed. For him the past was obviously well behind him.

'Anna, maybe it's a pipe dream,' he told her. 'It came to me on the way here, from something Carla said and from Victoir's plans. But it'd take someone with a massive social conscience.'

'And how can a Castlavaran have a social conscience?' It was an angry mutter.

'You've said you're not a Castlavaran.'

'You don't believe that—or is your memory still selective?' She glowered and then decided to be honest. To lay it all out there.

'Leo, from the moment you told me you couldn't marry me, you acted like you could hardly remember that my name is Raymond. I remember, though, and it still hurts. I know it's stupid, but there it is. I even talked to our clinic's psychologist about it. How needful was that? She says it's tied up with my father walking away, my mother rejecting me over and over—and then you doing the same thing. She says I need to focus forward, not backward. So now... You judging me on my mother's name looks backward to me. Leo, you've checked I'm not dying. I assume you've routed Victoir because he's not here with his horrid documents. So what's left? You can trust me with your pipe dream or you can leave. Take your pick.'

'Anna—'

'Just do it, Leo.'

He closed his eyes and she could see him almost visibly brace himself.

When he opened them again he'd changed. His look was one of pure challenge.

'As you like,' he said formally, as if what he was about to say was business and nothing more. What had been between them in the past was—of course—once again to be forgotten. He sat again so he could talk to her at eye level.

Doctor to patient? Not so much.

'So here it is,' he said. 'I believe it's possible.

Within the terms of the Trust you have a chance to do something spectacular.'

'What?' She wasn't bemused. She was still just plain angry.

'You could turn part of this castle into a hospital. You could provide a base for us to expand and the facilities for us to give first-class treatment. You could be the first Castlavaran who cares. You could prove me—and all of this island—wrong.'

CHAPTER FIVE

To say she was hornswoggled was an understatement.

'A hospital.' She managed to say it but it was a word, not a concept.

'I know,' he said, gently now, as if he still thought she was ill. 'It's a crazy idea. I guess you're either a Castlavaran, in which case you've had greed and indolence bred into you, or you're an English doctor who wants nothing to do with your inheritance because it's twenty years until you can claim it. Either way, Tovahna is the loser. I'm sorry, Anna. I didn't mean to throw this at you tonight. But I just said…'

'Yeah,' she said, dazed. 'You just said…'

'It's something you could think about when you go back to England,' he said. Could she hear a sliver of hope?

'But…' She shook her head and winced. 'First of all you're still being insulting. I'm either greedy or I don't care. And if I'm neither of those then I'll fall on what has to be a preposterous plan. Turn a castle into a hospital?' Oh, her head hurt.

These weeks since she'd heard of this incredible inheritance hadn't been wasted. She'd learned more of Tovahna than she'd believed possible. She knew the poverty that had kept the people in their places for a thousand years. But Martin and his colleagues had also checked the terms of her inheritance. They'd found it rigidly structured so the heir couldn't make changes.

Money was to be spent for the maintenance of the castle or the welfare of the incumbent. For nothing else.

Incumbent. That was her.

In twenty years maybe she could hand the vast wealth over to some central agency, gift people their own land, do some good. But not before that. Martin had spelled it out.

'The Trust's in the hands of a firm of conservative lawyers in Milan. It'll provide you with a sweet income but there's nothing more to be done for years. Stay home and wait.'

'How...?' she said now, in a small voice because speaking of such a thing seemed so immense, so impossible that even saying it aloud was ludicrous. 'How could I turn the castle into a hospital? How could I possibly fit that around the terms of the Trust?'

And it seemed Leo had an answer.

'The same way Victoir's proposing converting the place into apartments,' he told her. 'The way he's proposing getting around the Trust is that you'd nominally have one set aside for your personal use, and the others would be deemed as being built for your guests. Your guests would pay a hefty price for the privilege but that wouldn't matter. They'd be here for your pleasure. So a hospital…'

'You're saying I could use a hospital? Have the hospital for my own personal use? I'd need to bump my head once a day. More.'

He didn't smile. The intent look didn't fade.

'That wouldn't work. There's no way that'd fit the terms of the Trust. What could work…' Once again, a deep breath, as if what he was about to say was so huge he could scarcely believe he was saying it. And when he finally said it, she could understand why.

'The only way it could work was if this hospital itself was your life,' he said. 'You'd need to live here—really live here—and the hospital would need to be as important to you as the over-the-top sports cars your cousin used to collect. They're gathering dust in the massive garages he had built for them. He could hardly use them because the roads here are so bad. With a little gumption he could have had the roads repaired so he could use them—that would have helped the islanders and been within the terms of the Trust—but that would have taken sense he didn't have. But, Anna, if your passion, your life was a medical centre, to serve not only you but this whole island, then the lawyers in Milan must surely agree. But you would need to live here. Make Tovahna your home. Be the first Castlavaran in generations to make a difference to your people.'

'My people.'

'They are your people.'

'I'm *not* a Castlavaran.' How many times did she have to say it?

'Don't quibble, Anna,' he said roughly, and she thought she detected emotion underlying the tone. How? Because she knew this man. She knew him so well...

Yet she didn't know him at all. He was a stranger, and he was suggesting the preposterous.

What was he asking? He wanted her to stay here, by herself, with the beastly Victoir. He wanted her to forget everything that had happened between the pair of them. He wanted... the impossible.

'I want to go home.' It was a childish thing to say but it was what came out when she opened her mouth. And Leo looked at her as if it was what he'd expected all along.

'Of course you do. Run back to England with your inheritance and forget about us. Well, at least I've tried.'

'You call that trying?' The words were out before she could stop them as anger surged, a swift and unexpected response to his look of disgust.

'What do you mean?' His voice was cold and that made her angrier.

Her legs were dangling over the edge of the stupid over-the-top bed. Her feet were bare. Despite her pink and purple, she felt exposed. Vulnerable.

And still angry.

'I mean I've just been hit on the head,' she managed. 'I'm still tired and headachy. I'm also coming to terms with an inheritance that's made me feel like I've been hit by a sledgehammer. A golden sledgehammer, agreed, but a sledgehammer regardless. Add to that I'm confronted by an ex-fiancé who hurt me. I'm stuck in a thousand-year-old castle that feels like the set of a gothic movie. Plus I have a creepy administrator who comes in here with his indecipherable documents and who takes me underground without a hard hat and almost kills me, just to prove it's dangerous so I'll sign his documents fast. Yeah, I get that, I'm not stupid. And he doesn't even knock when he comes into my bedroom. So now you say I should turn the castle into a hospital and I say I want to go home and you act like what else could be expected of a rich, indolent, money-grubbing Castlavaran? Well, I'm not even a Castlavaran and, Leo Aretino, you can take your castle and your hospital and you can stick it!'

And she picked up one of her massive down-filled pillows and hurled it at him.

It hit him on the chest and slid harmlessly to his knees.

He placed it aside as if it was nothing and she glared and wanted the floor to open and swallow her.

Or Leo.

He was in her bedroom. In her chair.

He was far, far too close.

'Get out,' she said.

'I may just have put my case badly.'

'I don't care. Get out.'

The door opened.

Victoir.

'Get out,' she said again, only this time it was said in unison—with Leo—and it was the break they needed. Or she needed.

Nothing like a common enemy.

'I just…' Victoir started, and she decided it was about time she stopped being Victoir's doormat. Wasn't he her employee? Whatever, at least she could direct some of her pent-up frustration at him.

'You didn't knock. Basic rules, Victoir. Please leave.'

'If the doctor's finished…'

'He hasn't finished. He's explaining something to me that I wish to have explained. He'll see himself out when he's done. Please close the door behind you, and if you walk into my bedroom again without knocking I'll ask the lawyers in Milan to have you removed by yesterday.'

He stared at her and she faced him down.

He left. Fast.

'Wow,' Leo said, as Victoir disappeared and the heavy door was tugged closed. 'Well done. Hey, you really are a Castlavaran.'

'Don't. You'll get me started again.'

'I'm sorry.' He sighed. 'But you're right. You have far too much on your plate for me to be loading you with more.'

'Is that all you're sorry for?'

'You must know it's not,' he said gently. 'Anna, I've been sorry for a very long time.'

And that pretty much silenced her.

The silence stretched on. She was looking at him, seeing strain. She was waiting, but she didn't know what she was waiting for. What she was hoping?

'I'm sorry for not explaining,' he said at last.

'Explaining your hospital scheme? There's still time.'

'No,' he said softly. 'For not explaining ten years ago. For being nineteen and being hopelessly in love and then being dumbstruck by learning who your mother was. For not being able to explain it to you then. For being young and stupid and even cruel. For not being able to control my own hurt to ease yours. I still believe that I had no choice, but most of all, Anna, I'm deeply, deeply sorry that I had to walk away.'

The words left her winded.

After all these years…to have him finally say it.

She felt like a long-faded scar had suddenly split, to reveal there was still infection deep within.

Her psychologist had given her strategies for not looking back. Where was her psychologist now, when she was most needed? Strategies… She couldn't think of a single one.

'You didn't want…' she started, but he shook his head.

'Anna, you have no idea how much I wanted.'

'How can I know that? One minute we were planning marriage and then nothing.'

'I should have asked before. About your mother.'

'My mother was nothing to do with our relationship. She had very little to do with me. I told you she was a wild child. I told you there was man after man after man. What else was there to say?'

'That she was a Castlavaran?'

'As far as I was concerned, she was Katrina Raymond. She'd married my father, even if the marriage ended before I was born. I told you she'd been unhappy at home and her mother had died. I told you everything I knew.'

The only time she'd learned more had been the night she'd introduced Katrina to Leo.

She hadn't seen her mother for almost a year. Katrina had been in the States, but had breezed back to London and decided to drop in on her daughter.

'My head-in-her-books daughter has a man? Well, well, let's meet him.'

She'd been reluctant. To say she and her mother were dysfunctional would have been an understatement.

Anna had always been cared for—sort of. Katrina had access to money. 'It's family money, sweetheart—money's the only thing they're good for.' There'd been funds for an apartment with nannies, while Katrina had been off doing what she wanted. There'd been money to support Anna to study. There'd been no mother love.

Neither had there been any sense of history. Katrina wouldn't talk of home. 'There's some sort of Trust set up so my father has to support me,' she'd told her. 'That's all you need to know. He's an appalling man, Anna. Don't ask.'

So she hadn't asked, and the only part of Tovahna she knew was the language, taught to her in the times Katrina returned to the apartment to get over her latest love affair or to escape from whatever disaster she was in.

Anna had tried to warn him. 'She's unstable, Leo. She'll talk too fast. She'll come across as sophisticated and brittle but underneath...'

Underneath there were scars that Anna could only guess at. And then that night at dinner, the scars were exposed for all to see.

Maybe it was Leo's gentleness. His kindness. His perception? Even at nineteen he knew how to empathise, and Katrina was captivated.

He spoke to Katrina in Tovahnan and maybe that had been the undermining of Katrina's defences.

'So tell me about your father?' he asked Katrina at last, when the pizza had been replaced by coffee. 'My father died early, but my mother still lives on Strada Del Porto on the island's east side. Is that anywhere near where your father lives?'

What followed was a loaded silence, and

Anna looked at her mother in astonishment and thought, Is she about to crack? She'd hardly talked of her father, even to her. But then…

'As far as I know, my father still lives in that great gothic castle he loves so much,' she said, in a voice that was almost a whisper. 'It's the only thing he loves. He sits there and pretends to be a king and he's cared for nothing and for no one. Not my mother, and not me. And my brother's just like him. They can rot in their castle for all I care.'

And Leo stared at her in blank astonishment. 'You're a Castlavaran…'

'Don't say that name.'

'But he's your—'

'Enough.' Katrina pushed back her chair and walked out of the restaurant.

And that was that. One ring returned. One love affair over.

'I was so immature,' Leo said now, and it was so much what she thought that she blinked.

'Well. Good of you to admit it.'

'I should have explained.'

'So should my mother. I'm putting her in the same category. Let's keep Anna in ignorance and let her face the consequences without warning, without respect, without any acceptance of the fact that I had a right to know.'

'Anna…'

'My grandfather and my uncle and then my cousin were all self-serving creeps. I know that now. My mother was a brittle, damaged alcoholic. I know that, too. And you added that up and decided I must be more of the same and you'd cut me out of your life before I could contaminate you.'

'It was much, much more than that.'

'How would I know? Neither of you had the courtesy to explain.'

'I thought your mother—'

'I'd already said she'd told me nothing. She died four years ago, still having told me nothing.'

Unbidden, the hurt of so many years was spilling out, fury at her mother mixed with fury at Leo. But it was crazy, dumb, useless. It was adolescent anger, hurt from a time she should have put behind her.

She understood now, or she thought she did. After that night she'd done her own investigation into her mother's family and she even understood why Leo had walked away. Sort of.

'If I'd stayed with you I could never have come home again,' he said. 'I knew that.'

'And coming home was everything.'

'It was.' He hesitated. 'Hell, Anna, I should have spelled it out. I know that. But this country…you're getting a sense now of how impoverished we are. To send me to London to do medicine…it was a huge deal for the islanders. My father was dead and my mother had no means of support. I should have gone fishing when I was twelve, but my teachers told the town how smart I was. To be honest, most smart kids leave the island as soon as they can but I couldn't walk away from my mother for ever, and the islanders knew it. So when I said I wanted to be a doctor, somehow they managed it. I still don't know how. Because of the draconian rule of your family, every cent had to be accounted for.'

'But they never have been my family,' she managed, and he held up his hands, the same way he'd held them up ten years ago. Warding her off.

'Anna, I've said I'm sorry. I'm also sorry for being too immature to explain properly, for walking away so fast. But to be honest, maybe it was for the best, getting it over with fast.' He hesitated. 'I hope you did get over it fast. You have a partner now?'

What was there to say to that? A woman had some pride. 'Don't kid yourself that I've mourned you for ten years,' she told him, attempting to glower. 'I've had a very good time. I have a great job, a lovely home, dogs. I started dating Martin two years ago. He's a lawyer and a friend, and he'd be here in a flash if I asked him. As would any number of my friends.'

'But not now that you're injured?'

'I have a sore head, not a cerebral bleed. And you…' Two could play at his game. 'Wife? Kids? Goldfish?'

'I'm too busy for relationships,' he said brusquely. 'Moving on. Anna, the idea of the hospital…you're saying no.'

She hesitated. She was trying hard to be grown up, she told herself. She needed to shelve her adolescent self. She needed to get over a pain that surely should be well gone.

A hospital. Here.

Martin's advice had been sound. 'Do nothing. You can spend twenty years planning what to do when you finally inherit. Just go and look and then come home.'

Home sounded infinitely appealing.

But so did doing something. Something splendid?

'I didn't say no,' she said, slowly now, thinking it through. If she could get over the past, if she could see how this could happen… If she could get over how this man made her feel…

'Tell you what,' she said, pushing herself to her feet again. And once again she wobbled and needed to let Leo take her arm to steady her. Regardless. 'I'm rested,' she said. 'Yes, I'm still a bit shaky but I'm okay. Let's put…let's put everything behind us. You know this castle?'

'I have been in it,' he said. 'I was your cousin's treating doctor.'

'So you've been in his bedroom and in the entrance. Anywhere else?'

'I knew a lot of it as a boy,' he admitted. 'Your uncle ran on a skeleton staff so we could sneak around undetected. As kids…we did do our own exploring.'

'Well, there you go,' she said, determinedly cheerful. Determined to let bygones be bygones. Determined not to let the feel of his hand on her arm make her feel…what she needed to be long over feeling. 'You know it, and you've obviously thought this through. So, Dr Aretino. Let's forget the girlfriend-boyfriend thing. Let's also forget the doctor-patient thing. We're medical colleagues and you have a medical-based proposal. Let's take a walk through this castle. My castle,' she amended, because she was still getting her head around it and if she was going to face Victoir down then she needed the authority. And it wouldn't hurt if this man held her at a distance either.

'Victoir's shown me Yanni's over-the-top apartments and he's shown me through sections that are obviously dangerous,' she told him. 'But I know he has his own agenda. *Let's turn what we can into more opulence and knock the rest down*, is the gist of what he's telling me. So, Dr Aretino, let's go for a tour and you can tell me how any other option would be possible.'

CHAPTER SIX

HE'D DREAMED OF this since he was twelve years old. The night his father had died he'd stood sobbing under the shadow of the massive castle. That night of tears had matured into a vow to create a medical service equal to any in the world—or at least a medical service to stop islanders dying needlessly, uselessly, heartbreakingly.

He hadn't succeeded. Sure, he'd done a lot. He'd got through medical school. He and Carla had badgered the Castlavarans to give enough to provide basic services for themselves, and they'd organised islander contributions. He'd used contacts he'd made during training to plead for donations from abroad. They'd achieved a basic needs hospital with basic needs facilities.

But there wasn't enough staff, enough equipment, enough of anything.

'I need to get my head around the present situation,' Anna was saying. She'd put on shoes and socks. They were heading out from her room into the start of the endless corridors leading…well, he knew where. Anna clearly didn't.

He had his hand under her arm. He wasn't sure whether she needed it but she wasn't pulling away, and he wasn't about to let go.

'What do you want to know?' he asked.

'Everything,' she said expansively. 'But for a start… Why don't you have enough doctors?'

'We have no university on the island.' He hesitated. 'More than that. If we scrape to send one of our students to med school they're offered jobs overseas that are far more lucrative than here. Six years away…they learn to like things that the island can't offer.'

'And sometimes they fall in love and stay,' she said, and he winced. Hell, he'd like to turn back time.

He couldn't. 'As you say,' he said formally.

'So the hospital…'

'We had no funds to build from new. We've knocked four houses into one.'

'Which explains why it's a rabbit warren.'

'We had no choice. Every islander is eking out a precarious existence on what land they have. There are no central open spaces and no money to build.'

And then they turned the last passage to the door that opened to the great hall.

Which was…great.

Leo had been in here once when he was eight years old. He and his mates had burrowed through the tunnels and emerged to explore.

Here they'd stopped, so gobsmacked that they'd forgotten caution. One of the Castlavaran retainers had found them and thrown them out.

He'd thought, over the years, that his impression must have been influenced by his size. Everything looked huge to an eight-year-old.

But it was vast. Columns soared three storeys high to a vaulted ceiling. There was a massive stone-tiled floor. The walls were covered by enormous tapestries, frayed and faded.

The focus point was a fireplace, and what a fireplace. It took up half the end wall. Blackened by fires from the ages, it reeked of history.

'Victoir's plans have this down as a central gymnasium and swimming pool for the apartments,' Anna said, conversationally. As if it was of no import at all. 'So what would you do with it in your plan? I can hardly see it divided into individual wards. Nurses' station perhaps?'

He smiled. It was the first time he'd felt like smiling for days, and the sensation was…okay.

But he was here on a mission. Focus, he told himself.

'A swimming pool would be a great idea,' he said, forcing his voice to sound calm. To not sound eager instead. 'Can you imagine this place as a rehab centre? A pool, walking routes, grab bars around the walls, ball games, nets and loops, whatever… Right now, if islanders are injured we scrounge enough to get them off the island for immediate treatment. But the cost of overseas rehab is out of the question, so they come back and we do the best we can. But here… Anna, can you imagine what this place would look like?'

He hesitated, catching his passion and corralling it. 'Sorry. I'm way ahead of myself. Setting this place up as a hospital will be costly enough without adding swimming pools. I'm not hoping for the world, just a working hospital.'

'Maybe,' she said non-committally. 'Show me more.'

So he did. Victoir didn't show his face. The small number of servants employed for upkeep were nowhere to be seen.

Leo had seen the rooms used by Anna, and

before her by members of her family. He'd been here to treat Yanni for his many complaints, real and imagined. Those rooms were so opulent they were enough to make him recoil in distaste. Staff rooms opening onto the courtyard were clinical, neat and serviceable, but they were a tiny percentage of the castle space.

The rest, seen now for the first time since his childhood exploring, was a vast mishmash of different styles, different tastes, different generations. Dust sheets shrouding ancient furniture. Ancient drapes and wallpaper hung in tatters. Plaster split, cracked, falling. He could see rising damp.

He found himself growing more discouraged as they went from floor to floor, from room to room. The corridors were ill lit, with single light bulbs sparsely spaced. Most of the rooms were lit by the same single bulb, many with frayed, dangling cords. He thought of what it would cost to update the electrics and the thought made him feel ill.

Victoir's idea of apartments might get itself past the trustees as there'd be money coming in, but what he was proposing was surely out of the question. Rooms would have to be knocked together, lifts put in, the whole place practically gutted.

They walked from room to room, from level to level, silent. When he started to speak Anna shushed him.

'Victoir gave me a quick tour on my first day here,' she said. 'He talked all the time, about his apartment plans. About them being the only option. He's pushing me to do it urgently, telling me the place is falling down. I cracked my head over his plans. Let me take time to absorb yours.'

But Leo no longer had plans. As they opened each door the plans faded further and further from the realms of the possible.

Finally they emerged to the vast circle of parapets, to the walkway around long-unused battlements. To a moonlit view that enveloped the whole island, outward to the faint outline of Italy beyond.

This view, and the pristine beach below, long protected by castle walls, were the reason Victoir envisaged apartments for the super-rich, Leo thought. They'd flock here, to an untouched, luxury, Mediterranean retreat. It'd be historic, fascinating, available to only the feted few.

Instead of a hospital.

But his enthusiasm had disappeared. By the time they reached the battlements he was accepting its impossibility. The cost... How could he even have thought it?

The last hint of sunset was fading in the west, casting a faint tangerine hue over the ocean. A lone fishing boat was coming into harbour, its wake a translucent wash. While he stood silently by Anna's side, accepting the impossibility of what he'd dreamed, a pod of dolphins started surfing its wake.

'Imagine recuperating here,' Anna said, finally speaking but talking almost to herself. 'The island's elderly in the nursing home part of that dump you call a hospital... Imagine them up here with the sun on their faces.'

'We can't do it,' he said heavily as the hopelessness of his proposal sank home. 'Now that I've seen the place again... I'm sorry I even suggested it.'

She turned away from watching the dolphins and stared at him. 'Why not?'

'Apart from Yanni's apartments I haven't been in the castle since I was a kid,' he conceded. 'Maybe I was looking at it through rose-coloured glasses, or maybe my memory's played me false.

I did remember the great hall. I was imagining it as a major cost, digging out a swimming pool, setting it up for rehab. I knew that was a pipe dream but the rest…a basic hospital… I thought that if your Trust could cover the capital costs we might be able to do it. But tonight… Anna, I see what Victoir means. This place is impossible. To do it up would cost a king's ransom.'

'I have a king's ransom,' she said, and for a moment he thought he'd misheard.

'Anna…'

'Just how much do you think I inherited?' She leaned on the parapet. The dolphins were practically turning handstands behind her but she was focussed on him.

'I have no idea,' he said faintly. 'It's none of my business.'

'If most of that money's been accrued via the poverty and misery of the islanders, then it's very much your business.'

'That's been going on for generations.'

'It has,' she agreed. 'As far as I can see, the lords of this castle or whatever they called themselves have had Miser as a middle name for generations. Early on they apparently spent their rent roll paying mercenaries to protect their stronghold from the marauding hordes, but the hordes seem to have given up long since. But the family didn't relax. The Castlavarans seem to have been saving as if the hordes are still about to attack again. Martin insisted we get an accounting of the entire estate and now I have a number. So…take a deep breath, Dr Aretino, and listen.'

So he took a deep breath and listened.

And the figure…

She said it once and then she had to say it again. It was too immense, too breathtaking, to respond to.

Out to sea the dolphins gave up their acrobatic display in disgust. Neither Anna or Leo noticed.

'I can't…' Leo said at last, and Anna nodded.

'Neither can I. It's left me hornswoggled. But I didn't think I could do much for twenty years. Restore the castle, yes. Turn it into apartments even. Anything else, no.'

'But…'

'But now you've shown me another way. The Trust is clear. I can spend anything I like on my personal use. The lawyers in Milan say if I want to collect diamonds, as long as I keep them in the castle then that's fine by them. So if I want to create the hospital of my dreams for my personal satisfaction, what's the difference?' She took a deep breath. 'The trustees seem staid, conservative but they have no interest in preventing me doing something like this. Their role is to stick to the letter of the Trust. I'll ring Martin and—'

'Martin...'

'I told you. He's a lawyer and a good one.'

Martin. His thoughts seemed to be jerked sideways.

What Anna was proposing was the stuff of dreams and why a guy called Martin should be getting in the way of his thoughts...

He wasn't here with her. Surely if they were serious he'd be here.

Not important. Not! He fought his way back to what she was saying. What she was thinking.

'You'd really do this,' he said slowly.

'I think,' she said, just as slowly, 'that I might have a responsibility to do it. I could set this up as a state-of-the-art hospital. More. If I really can do anything for my personal use—as long as it's within my remit as castle resident—then my head's starting to spin with possibilities.'

'Anna...'

'Don't stop me,' she begged. 'This is full-on fantasy and I'm enjoying myself. What else? I like travelling to neighbouring countries but I don't like flying. So, yes, I need a helicopter based here for when I'm in a hurry—and, incidentally, for patients who need evacuation to medical facilities even we can't provide. But for my normal day-to-day pleasure I'd like a ferry, one big enough for me not to feel seasick. And the trustees should surely not object if I save costs by letting the locals use it as well. And visiting tourists. Day trippers from the mainland.'

She was off and running, her mind obviously tumbling with ideas. 'The hospital staff...' she said. 'You say you can't keep doctors? I like doctors and I like them living around me. They're my friends and I don't like living in this castle by myself. If we set up accommodation, use some of Victoir's ideas, I could surely entice and pay for the best specialists. They could come and teach me—and, of course, anyone else who's on my payroll...'

'You're making me dizzy.'

'I'm making me dizzy,' she conceded.

She paused. They both paused.

'I've gone from thinking I can do nothing to thinking I can do everything,' she said at last.

'I need to talk to Martin but if I can get around the Trust…'

There he was again. Martin. Why did it shake him out of his fantasy, remind him of reality?

'You'll never do it,' he said, and she blinked.

'Why not?'

'Because you'd have to live here.'

She turned to stare out to sea again, and he could almost see cogs whirring. He should stop her, he thought. She'd been hit on the head. She shouldn't make any decisions yet.

She wasn't intending to, he reminded himself. She was going to talk to a lawyer called Martin.

'I'll need my dogs,' she said at last.

'Would you need Martin?'

That hauled her out of her train of thoughts. She turned to him, eyes flashing sudden anger. 'Butt out of that, right now.'

'Anna…'

'What happens here, the plans for this castle, this hospital, this island… I'll need advice and collaboration. But the personal stuff… You lost the right when you walked away ten years ago.'

'I've said—'

'You're sorry. And that's fine. I'm over a teen-aged romance and you should be, too.'

But he had to say it. The night… This woman…
'Anna, the way I feel—'

'Don't you dare,' she snapped. 'Finish that train of thought right now. Moving on. Do you want to be in charge of setting up a hospital to tick the boxes of every islander's basic needs?'

'You wouldn't want me in charge.'

'I'm not a fool, Leo.' Her voice was still cold. 'Basic as it is, from what I've seen, you run your current hospital well. You know the islanders' needs so I'll need your help. I imagine we'll need expert assistance, advice from people who know how to set up the kind of state-of-the-art medical facilities we're talking about. Architects. Heritage advisors too, because my head's starting to think beyond medicine. The tunnels Victoir wants me to close… If they were open to the public…made safe, and with guided tours… We could charge entrance fees to mainlanders coming over on my new ferry. The trustees surely would see the sense in that—spending money to make money. We could even set this up as a hub for international visitors…'

'You think you might be getting carried away?'

'I definitely am,' she said, and she smiled, and suddenly the coldness was gone. This was a great, warm, happy smile, a smile he hadn't seen for...ten years?

A smile that was no longer aimed at him but at a project that was obviously entrancing her.

Entrancing. It was a good word. No, it was a great word.

It described her exactly. An injured colleague, a woman in pink and purple yoga gear, what was left of unruly copper curls, the rest of her head covered with an oversized dressing.

She still had freckles. He wanted to touch those freckles.

'We're running away with ourselves,' he managed, struggling to take the personal out of a situation that held the fate of practically the entire island in its grasp. 'The lawyers in Milan...'

'I'll have Martin speak to them. I can't imagine why I haven't thought of this before.'

'It's only weeks since Yanni died,' he said. 'I imagine you've been in shock.'

'I have,' she admitted. 'One minute I was a nice normal family doctor in a nice normal English village—and suddenly I was an heiress responsible for...' She shrugged. 'Okay, I wasn't sure what I was responsible for until I came here, and Victoir's attempt to make me see the place was dangerous led to a split head. Which led to you.' She hesitated. 'So I guess the split head's lucky. Because it led to you, it led to me thinking outside the box.' But then, as if events had suddenly overwhelmed her, she put her hand to her head and her smile faded.

And instantly he turned back into what he should have been all along. Anna's doctor. Nothing else.

'You need to be back in bed.'

'How can I sleep?'

'I guess you can't. I surely won't be able to. But you need to rest. Anna, this is all supposition until you run it past the trustees. And to stay here… It's a big decision. You'll need to run it past… Martin?'

'And the trustees,' she agreed. 'Mostly the trustees. But also my dogs. My dogs are very fussy about where they live.'

'And Martin?'

'Butt out, Leo.'

He held his hands up. 'Consider me butted. Sorry.'

'But you keep butting in again.' She gazed at him for a long moment, appearing to consider. 'Okay, if we're butting…tell me about you.'

'It's…'

'If you tell me it's none of my business I'll call Victoir.'

'What do you want to know?'

'Like, do you live alone? You say you haven't had time for a relationship. None at all? I find that hard to believe.'

'I live with my mother and her canary called Pepe.'

'Your mother…'

'She's ill. She's been ill for a long time.' Why had he told her that?

'I'm sorry.' A furrow appeared on her forehead. He remembered that furrow. *He liked that furrow.* 'Is that another reason you look so strained? Is there anything I can do?'

It took only that. He'd treated her appallingly and here she was, saying maybe she could spend her inheritance giving Tovahna a medical service that made his eyes water just to think about it. And now she was offering to help with his mother's care?

'She has multiple sclerosis,' he said simply. 'My aunt helps me with her care. Anna, it's me who should be sorry. The way I acted—'

'Was too long ago to be dredged up again and

again. Moving on, Leo… Yes, I need to rest. To-morrow I'll think again.' Her hand went back to her head. 'I ache,' she said simply. 'I need to lie down.'

'Of course you do.' She turned toward the stairs down from the parapets. The stone here was crumbling. He couldn't help himself—or more probably it was the sensible thing to do. He caught her arm and held, supporting her.

He half expected her to pull away. That she didn't…

Why did it make him feel light?

They reached the top of the stairs. Beneath them was gloom. His hold on her arm tightened.

But she paused. Once again he thought she'd pull away, but instead she turned and gazed back over the stonework, over the moonlit sea. An old man was fishing on a low stone jetty jutting out from just in front of the castle walls. While they watched, the line bent. He reeled it in, held it up for a moment.

'Squid,' Leo said softly. 'Luigi and Sondra will have calamari for dinner.'

'You know all the islanders?'

'Pretty much. I'm their doctor. My father was

a fisherman and I have relatives all over the island. They trust me.'

There was another admission. Personal.

They trust me.

Why had he said it? Because it was important, he thought. Trust was the reason he'd had to come home. It was the reason he couldn't ever have stayed with this woman.

But now she was here…

It was just as impossible, he thought. The heiress to the Castlavaran fortune? No and no and no.

'Leo…'

'Hmm…?' He was still watching Luigi. The fisherman had caught what he needed. He was now packing up his ancient fishing gear, heading home.

He needed to head home, too. Check on his mother. Head back to the hospital.

'It was good between us, wasn't it?'

That was a blindsider. What had she just said? What had been between them was too long ago to be dredged up again, but here she was…dredging?

Or simply putting it out there?

'It was,' he admitted. 'And I'm sorry it had to end like it did.'

'I still don't get it,' she admitted. 'But I'm starting to think...people can change. You've changed.'

'I don't think I have.'

'You care.'

'I always cared.'

'Not for me, you didn't.'

'I did care, Anna.' And suddenly it was too much. She was gazing at him as if she wanted to see inside; as if she wanted to read his mind. Once upon a time he'd thought she could. 'Hell, I cared. I still care.'

'Leo...'

And what happened next he could never afterwards explain. He was tired. Stressed. The sudden appearance of Anna out of his past had jolted him. The crisis with Carla had shaken him even more. And now...the prospect of doing something amazing with this castle, the vista of a future he'd never dreamed might be possible... Yeah, they were all excuses but they weren't reasons. The reason was that Anna was standing on the castle steps and she was looking at him as he remembered her looking up at him ten years ago.

She'd changed. This was a mature version of the Anna he'd known and loved. She still had her glorious hair and her freckles. Her nose was still snub but the changes were subtle. Her eyes had laughter lines etched at the corners. She hadn't grieved for him too much, then, he thought, and then he thought, how arrogant was that?

But there was that something about her that said she didn't always smile. There was a maturity, a softness, a gentle sense of wisdom.

He remembered thinking all those years ago that she'd make a great family doctor and now he was sure of it.

He was also sure that she was just…great.

She was still looking at him. Asking unspoken questions.

Just looking.

She had a…what? Boyfriend? Partner? Where was this phantom Martin now?

Not here when he should be here.

So where was sense?

He should propel her gently down the stairs,

send her back to bed. He knew it. He should become her doctor again.

But her eyes were holding his.

The warmth. The soft wash of the waves beneath the castle. The night.

This was madness.

But, madness or not, it was as if the world held its breath, asking a question…

And the question had only one answer.

He kissed her.

One minute she was hesitating on the stairs, looking back at Leo, feeling confused.

More than confused. Disoriented. Discombobulated. Was there a bigger word? The way this man made her feel…

She'd put thoughts of him away, had made a life for herself, proved without a doubt that there had been a life after Leo.

But he was watching her now, his eyes troubled, his gaze acknowledging there was unfinished business.

If it was unfinished then she had to finish it. She had to turn away and make her way down the stairs to her ridiculous apartment. She had to close the door behind her, raise the drawbridge, pull in every defence at her disposal.

His hand was still on her arm.

She glanced down at it and then back to his face. His dark, questioning eyes. The look of… trouble?

She couldn't help herself. She raised her hand to his face and traced the harsh line of cheekbone. The touch made her feel…

She couldn't think how she felt.

He was so close.

Did she draw his face down to hers? She didn't know. All she knew was that her world seemed to empty of everything except the sight, the feel, the touch of this man.

And then he kissed her, and her world shorted.

Or that's what it felt like. An electric shock seemed to jar her entire system and then simply shut it down. It left room for nothing. Not one of the five senses was operating—or maybe they all were.

Taste… The way his mouth fused with hers. Glorious memories flooding back.

Smell… The faint smell of disinfectant, the smell every doctor knew so well. But more. He smelt of himself, a waft of arrant male testosterone.

Hearing… She could hear his breath. It was almost as if it was as one with hers.

Sight. Her eyes were filled with the vision of Leo, here, now.

Touch.

And there was the biggie, overriding all. The warmth of his hold, his strength, his tenderness… He was taking what he needed but giving back in spades.

Oh, this kiss… She had no defences from this kiss. The feel of him…the way her body moulded to his…

Somewhere, maybe in church, maybe in some long-forgotten romance novel, she'd read or she'd heard the words describing marriage as two becoming one. Ten years ago, aged all of nineteen, she'd fallen into this man's arms and had thought, yes. That's what this was.

Only of course it hadn't been that. They'd never been one. Over the years she'd reminded herself of the naïve kid she'd been. She'd told herself that marriage was for the long haul. It wasn't a romantic slogan. It was something you entered with your head as well as your heart.

She'd vowed never again to let herself be swept away by emotion, but here she was, subsumed by so much emotion she was drowning in it. This kiss was claiming her, and it was as if…she'd come home.

Only of course she hadn't. This was surely just an ex-boyfriend who'd messed with her past. She needed sense. Now!

She wasn't sure whether Leo pulled away or she managed it, but somehow reality surfaced. Somehow they were inches away from each other.

That knock on the head must have been a doozy, she decided. She was staring at him in dawning horror. 'We can't do this.' She clutched at shreds of dignity but they were nowhere to be found.

Back away, her head screamed. Leave.

'Besides,' she managed, 'you're my treating doctor. I'm concussed. Kissing me is unethical.'

'It's good, though,' he said, and he had the temerity to grin. But the grin was short-lived.

She saw it fade and thought, He's almost as disconcerted as I am.

'I'm sorry,' he said.

'We're both sorry.'

'I need to leave.'

'After you've taken me back to my room,' she said, and suddenly she was panicking. He couldn't just take her up to the battlements, kiss her senseless and abandon her. 'I have no idea where I am. Three storeys up, two parapets across…or is that two storeys up, three parapets…' She tried hard to make her voice light, trying to break through panic, which was only partly caused by the fact that she felt lost—in more ways than one. 'I don't want to inadvertently call on creepy Victoir.'

'He really is creepy?'

'He really is creepy.' Somehow she fought to make her voice sound normal. 'God's gift to women, that's his self-assessment. When I arrived he was already talking about the apartment idea, but it took him about two minutes to realise I wasn't married, and I didn't have two heads. I suspect he has the wedding already planned. Bedding me first, marrying my fortune second. *Ugh.*'

'Ugh, indeed. Would you like me to stay?'

That was another breath-taker. 'You're kidding

me, right? Reject Victoir and have you instead? I don't think so.'

'I'm not talking bedding,' he said, and propelled her gently into the stairwell. What had happened between them only minutes ago was, apparently, to be forgotten.

Like it had been forgotten ten years ago?

'I have work to do,' he said, brusquely now. 'But my aunt is staying with my mother tonight. I could come back and sleep somewhere close enough for you to call.'

Time to be honest? There seemed no choice. 'Leo, if I called and I was half-asleep and you came, I wouldn't be the least bit surprised at what might happen,' she admitted. 'Face it, Leo, we've got a thing.'

'A thing.'

'A childish attraction we both need to get over. Thanks but, no, thanks. I'll be fine.'

'What if I send one of our nurses over?' he asked. 'Any one of them would be thrilled for a chance to stay inside the castle. I'll tell Victoir I want observations to be continued—maybe I'm worried about your emotional state.'

'My emotional state...'

'Concussion's a dangerous thing.' They'd

reached the landing leading to the passage to her wing. He turned and faced her, smiling, slightly ruefully. 'What just happened was totally out of character, I'm sure. Probably a result of your accident.'

'It was dumb,' she snapped. She felt so disoriented.

'I agree,' he said.

And again she thought, He's too close, too male, too... Leo?

'I was just as dumb. But, Anna, can I send a nurse to stay with you?'

And she looked up into his face and saw concern. Real concern.

This was nonsense. Why was she suddenly blinking back tears?

'I would appreciate...company,' she managed, and he nodded.

'Sensible. I'll send Juana over as soon as I get back.'

'You won't be short-staffed without her?'

'She'll be off duty, here to sleep, but she'll love to see this place. I suspect you might need obs for the entire time you stay here, a different nurse each time.'

'And if I stay permanently?'

'That really is an option?'

She took a deep breath and turned to face outward, through the deep, narrow slit that was used to light the stairwell, or, in more dangerous times, to shoot arrows on marauders threatening to storm the castle.

This castle was ages old, a vast, abiding reminder of Tovahna's history. It was also a cache of Tovahna's wealth, kept from the island's residents because of the greed of a family she wanted nothing to do with.

But she was part of that family, the last surviving remnant.

She could walk away, live in luxury for twenty years and then sell to the highest bidder.

Or she could make a difference.

She turned back to Leo, this man she'd once trusted with her heart. She wouldn't do that again. She wasn't stupid.

But she did trust him…with everything else. This place could be a hospital? She could make a difference?

She thought fleetingly of her lovely little cottage back in England, her cosy life. To abandon everything to live in a castle…

To make a difference.

With Leo?

Dammit, just say yes.

'Yes,' she said, almost defiantly, and then she said it again, loudly, so her voice echoed up and down the stairwell. 'Yes, Leo, staying is an option. In fact, from this angle, with the trustees' consent, it looks like a certainty.' And then her voice wobbled again. What was she doing, making a decision like this so fast?

And he got it. 'You can't make a decision like this tonight,' he told her. 'Think about it. Talk to this... Martin.' And then he hesitated. 'Anna, let me take you out of here for a day.' His voice cut across her resolution and she thought... What?

'Out where?'

'To see what you'd be doing.' His voice was strange, grim even. It was as if he was struggling between fantasy and reality as well. Was he? She didn't know. Did she know anything?

'What do you mean?'

'I mean you need to go into this with your eyes wide open.' He said it almost reluctantly. 'You need to see the bigger picture. But not tomorrow,' he told her hurriedly. 'You need to rest. But maybe Saturday? Bruno and Freya will both be back at work by then, and there's no clinic. I could try for a day off. I'd like to show you the real Tovahna—the people you'll be helping if you decide to go ahead with…what you're proposing.'

And she thought, He's like me. He does still think it's fantasy. 'I think I've already decided,' she said, but that wobble was still there.

'Anna, you've been concussed,' he said, gently now. 'I can't let you make promises now. But in a few days, when your head's not aching… Anna, will you trust me to show you my island, to show you my people? To let you see how much these fantastic dreams could change lives? Give me a day.'

A whole day with Leo?

Oh, she felt fuzzy. She felt like she was floating in fantasy but she had enough sense to realise that what Leo was suggesting was sensible. She should make no promises tonight.

But a whole day…

Her big, warm, lovely Leo.

No. He wasn't hers. He was a colleague, nothing else. And if he was a colleague and nothing else, then why not?

'Saturday,' she said, before she could change

her mind. 'It sounds like a plan to me. A nice island tour and nothing else, Leo Aretino. And now thank you very much but I need to go to bed.'

CHAPTER SEVEN

TOVAHNA'S CASTLE HAD been built and fortified to defend the island from barbarians. If I'd been leading them I might have fought harder, Anna thought. This island was worth fighting for.

She was sitting in the passenger seat of Leo's ancient Fiat. The roads were appalling, a pot-holed mess, but decrepit roads and old cars couldn't detract from the beauty around her.

The coast road alone was enough to take her breath away. The sea was sapphire-blue, the cliffs were low, white stone or sandy, and there was bay after bay that screamed, *Stop, paddle or swim, now.*

They'd left the single row of shops that served the town, and were now on the sparsely popu-lated far side of the island. Ancient stone cottages were set far apart, but people were still around, working in the olive groves or in veggie gardens, mending nets on the beaches, walking along the road from farm to farm. Leo's faded red Fiat was obviously well known, because every islander waved or called as he came into view.

He waved back but he was mostly silent. Letting Anna see the place without a running commentary?

For which she was grateful. She felt ill at ease with this man but she did want to see the island. It would have felt petty to knock back his offer, especially since her alternative chauffeur was Victoir.

But she had to find words soon. It was as if he was waiting for her to take it in, waiting for her verdict.

'It's beautiful,' she said at last as they topped a crest and miles of olive groves and the sparkling sea beyond spread out before her. Masses of wild roses—a species apparently endemic to the island—lined the road sides, breathtakingly beautiful. 'I can understand why you wanted to come back.'

'Needed to come back,' he corrected her. 'Don't let the beauty fool you. It disguises desperate need. Anna, would you mind if we stopped for a few moments? Dino Costa's ninety and he's pretty much bedbound. If I could check on him now it might save me a trip next week. There's a cove below the house. You might like to sit on a rock and watch the water, or take a stroll.'

'Of course,' she said, and then said diffidently, 'Unless you need some help.' She thought of the elderly, housebound clients she'd treated in her years of family doctoring. Social contact was the best medicine. Sometimes an interesting visit could do more good than any medicine she could prescribe.

So say it. 'Unless you think Dino might like to meet me,' she added, and Leo flashed her a look of surprise.

There was a moment's silence, and then, 'You mean it?'

'If you think it could help.'

And he got it. She saw his faint smile. 'For Dino...meeting you? Not only would he love it, it'll bring in every neighbour to hear all about it. For Dino that'd be gold.' He hesitated. 'He won't be polite, though. If you can take it...'

She grinned at that. 'Hey, I'm a family doctor. I've coped with plenty of abusive patients in my time. Besides, I already know what the islanders think of me. Bring it on.'

So they stopped at an ancient stone cottage set back from the cliffs, surrounded by olive trees that looked as if they hadn't been tended for years. A mass of lemon trees crowded the back garden, loaded with unused fruit. The ground was rough and stony. Apart from the pervasive wild roses, any attempt at a garden had been abandoned long since and the little dog that emerged to greet them looked as dejected as the surroundings he obviously lived in.

But Leo obviously knew him. He knelt and fondled his ears, brushing debris from his dust-coloured coat.

'Hey, Zitto, how's your master today?'

The little dog wriggled his pleasure as he realised he knew this visitor. Tail now wagging, he led the way through the open back door into the house.

'Dino? Are you open for visitors?'

'Leo?' It was a quavering old voice, rising in response. 'Is that you?'

'It definitely is,' Leo called back. 'Dino, I've brought a guest to meet you. Anna Castlavara. Is it okay to bring her in?'

'The Castlavara? In my home? You're telling me lies, Leo Aretino.'

'See for yourself,' Leo said, and ushered Anna in before him.

The old man was seated in a rocker by the fire. The woodstove was burning fiercely, on a day when it was already hot, but Anna was accustomed to visiting houses of the very old. Heat was a medicine all on its own. He struggled to rise but she crossed quickly and stooped to take his hand.

'Don't get up on my account,' she told him. 'I'm just here as background while Dr Leo does his checks.'

'I'll make tea,' the old man said, sounding distressed. 'I should have...'

'Dino's accustomed to Victoir checking rent rolls,' Leo told her. 'He's not accustomed to actual visits from...'

'I'm not a Castlavaran,' she said, quickly before he could finish. 'Signor Costa, I may have inherited the castle but I'm Anna Raymond. Dr Anna Raymond.' She gazed around the kitchen, thinking of the fuss involved in making tea, but of this man's obvious need to be hospitable. Her eyes fell on an empty bottle on the table. There were similar bottles, cleaned and empty, stacked on a shelf, each with a handwritten name scrawled on the front, and there were a couple of full ones on the dresser. A home brew? Excellent.

'Hey, it's almost lunchtime. Could I ask… maybe a tiny limoncello? If you have it?'

It was like flicking a switch. The old man's eyes gleamed with delight. He hauled himself to his feet, pushing away Leo's hand as he instinctively went to help.

'I make it myself,' he told them. 'All my own lemons. Our own lemons. My grandfather went to Sorrento, many, many years ago. Took a job on a fishing boat. Off he went and no one heard of him for years and then back he came with nothing but a bag full of lemon root stock. Femminello St Teresa, the best lemon in the world. "It'll make our fortune," he said, and of course it didn't but maybe the best limoncello is enough.'

He was fumbling in the dresser, producing three dusty glasses—crystal. He wiped them off with a frayed dishcloth, then headed to the refrigerator. Out of the freezer came a bottle like the others—filled, though, with a clear, bright yellow liquid, and frosted over with ice.

Three tumblers full. He poured them with infinite care, struggling to keep his hand from shaking—but both Leo and Anna knew better than to offer to help. Finally he handed them over. He straightened and Anna could almost hear his back creaking with the effort.

'To you,' he said, and raised an unsteady arm. 'You can't be worse than those before you, girl.'

'I might even be better,' she suggested, tilting her glass in response and feeling the amazing tang of frozen lemon burst in her mouth. 'Like your limoncello…you mix local with imported and you get a whole new flavour. Signor Costa, this is the best limoncello I've ever tasted. You know, this island has now imported a brand-new Castlavaran. So, like your limoncello, who knows what you'll get from me?'

Afterwards Leo wanted to check an abscess and it was obvious her welcome didn't extend to sharing that. So she did what Leo had suggested. She found a rock and looked out over the bay.

Leo found her there twenty minutes later. He sat down beside her and did a little bay-watching himself.

'Thank you,' he said at last. 'That'll be all over the island by yesterday—that you deigned to approve his limoncello.'

'I've been trained on Mavis Donohue's raspberry cordial,' she told him. 'She calls it cordial but it's about ninety percent proof. A glass full of cordial, about a teaspoon of soda and she beams the whole time I drink it. Luckily for me—and for the rest of her visitors—she has glaucoma. She has the most amazing pot plants, which I'm sure are now about eighty percent proof themselves.'

'So rating of Dino's limoncello...'

'Dino's limoncello is a thousand times better. There was no way a pot plant was getting that.'

'And it made his day,' he said softly. 'Thank you, Anna.'

'I'm not all bad,' she said, disconcerted by the gentleness of his tone.

'I know that. Not even a tiny bit.'

'Except for...'

'Let's not go there,' he told her. 'It's too good a day. Plus there's a bottle of limoncello for you in the car. He said...and I quote... "It'll sweeten her up, boy, and if anything this island needs it's a Castlavaran with a sweetened heart."'

'I'm not a Castlavaran!'

'And yet you need to be. As Anna Raymond you can return to your life in England. As the Castlavaran you can do good here.'

'But still be treated as the Castlavaran.'

'You can't escape it.'

'No.' She stared sightlessly out at the sea and let her thoughts drift. And finally she let herself say it.

'You can't escape it either,' she said.

He frowned. 'I don't know what you mean.'

'I think you do. You say you walked away because your country would have rejected you if you'd stayed with me. What about your pride?'

'Anna...'

'Victoir told me,' she said. 'I know Victoir's a sleazebag, but he's useful for information. He was warning me against you, or thought he was. He said, "His family is dirt poor." He almost sneered it. "As a child he was ragged, living on charity. For him to demand entry to the castle, to try and lord it over us because he has medical qualifications... He's a nothing. Any approach by him...be warned. He's out for what he can get."'

'Did he really say that?'

'Pretty much.' She cheered up a little then, hauling herself back to here and now. After all, this was history they were speaking of. 'Out for what you can get? That's the last thing I'd think of you. But is that yet another reason you walked away—you were afraid of my fabulous wealth? Rags to riches and you chose rags?'

'Anna…'

'I suspect it's true,' she said. 'But more fool you. I didn't have riches. And how did you know Yanni wouldn't have twelve little Yannis before he died.'

'I was stunned,' he told her. 'I didn't know what to think.'

'And you were being noble as well as dumb.' She sighed. 'And, honestly, I concede. If you'd stuck around I might have sobbed and clung and done any number of the dumb things adolescents do when they're crazily in love. So maybe what you did was reasonable. Anyway, Leo, I've been thinking and I've decided… I forgive you.'

'You forgive me,' he said faintly, and she managed to dredge up a grin. And suddenly it was a real one.

It was a gorgeous day. The sun was shining on her face. The setting was fantastic. She'd just had a truly excellent glass of limoncello and a gorgeous guy was showing her around the island.

So get on with it, she told herself. Get on with your life.

'I know, nobility is my middle name,' she told

him, and chuckled. 'So, moving on. I have decided to stay here.'

'With Martin?'

Where had that come from? She was trying not to get personal, or trying to put personal behind her and here he was, heading right back to where she least wanted to be. To her love life.

But why not be honest? If she was to stay here…

She'd have her dogs. She'd have her amazing apartment. She needed to do something about Victoir but surely she could manage that. And moving on…there might be any number of gorgeous guys on this island.

Leo would be a colleague and maybe a friend. He could ask, she decided, but she needed to set boundaries.

'That's none of your business, and you know it isn't,' she told him. 'Okay, putting all our cards on the table, Martin is actually now my ex-boyfriend. He's also my lawyer. But that's the last time you ask such a personal question, Leo Aretino. If I'm to stay here for the next twenty years I need to make a life for myself. I think I've decided that I can even have a very good time if I try hard enough. Right now, Victoir's intensely interested in my love life and so, it seems, are you. Neither of you have the right. I don't think Victoir and I can ever be friends— in fact, I'm sure of it—but you and I need to be colleagues and if we try very hard I suspect we can be friends, too. So for now I'm nobly forgetting that you ever jilted me and I'm moving on. Are you prepared to move on, too?'

'I guess…' He seemed totally disconcerted.

'Then that's noble of both of us.' She rose and smiled down at him. 'Or sensible. Speaking of sensible, Dino's limoncello was surely an aperitif, meant to be served before lunch. And I'm hungry. Do we need to head back to town to eat?'

'There's a small *taverna* around the next headland.'

'Excellent,' she said, and she smiled her very widest smile. Goading him to smile with her. 'Let's move on, then, shall we? Let's start being sensible from this moment on.'

Everything she'd said was totally, absolutely sensible. She'd pretty much summarised what had happened between them. She knew his reasons. She'd decided not to hold it against him.

They could move ahead as colleagues and as

friends, Leo thought, which was surely the very best of outcomes, so why did things still seem out of kilter?

The *taverna* he'd taken her to was one of his favourite places. Sofia made the best pasta on the island and Giuseppe surely caught the best calamari. Four small tables sat under their olive trees, looking out over the rickety jetty where Giuseppe tied his boat, and there were two tables inside if you were ever crazy enough not to want the view. They wanted the view and today they were the only customers. The menu was one dish, pasta with seafood, but the restricted menu was not a problem.

'Oh, my…' Anna was holding a sliver of squid for inspection before dispatching it forthwith. 'I've never eaten anything so good. Tell me I've died and gone to heaven.'

'It's not all hardship in this place,' he agreed. 'Pasta, olives, tomatoes, seafood…what's not to love?'

'The chef back at the castle seems to cook out of tins,' she said, sighing her pleasure. 'I was thinking twenty years in this place could be torture, but there's this! Hey, I'm a Castlavaran.

Surely I can command Sofia to come to my castle and cook for me.'

She'd spoken in Tovahnan. Giuseppe and Sofia had been watching them from the doorway. Three of their children, about twelve, ten and eight, had been running races down to the jetty and back.

As they heard what Anna said they stilled as one, turning to stare at her in consternation.

And Anna stared back, from one to the other. Her face lost all its colour as she realised what they were thinking.

'No! Oh, no, I was joking.' She rose and crossed to where Sofia was standing, so shocked she'd started shaking.

This was why things were still out of kilter, Leo thought. A friend and colleague? She was, but she was still the Castlavaran.

Leo had introduced her to the little family as they'd arrived and they'd reacted with awe. Now he saw Sofia try to back away in fear as Anna approached.

But Anna would have none of it. She held out her hands, grasping Sofia's workworn hands in hers and holding them tight.

'Sofia, that was a joke and a stupid one at that. I won't command anything.'

'You can take away our house,' Sofia said, sounding desperate.

'I can't.'

'You can take away anything you please on this island,' Leo told her. 'It is…yours to command.'

'I won't command anything.'

'It'll take time to prove that to the islanders.'

She looked back at him, dismayed. 'How?'

'It'll take time, that's all,' he said.

'Time. Twenty years?'

'I guess that's what you're committing.'

'I guess I am.' She turned back to Sofia. 'Sofia, please believe me when I say I'm threatening nothing. I may be your landlord but I have no intention of interfering with your lives. I'd like… if possible…to help Dr Leo to build a medical clinic to help all the island, and in time…given trust, maybe I could be a friend?'

But Sofia gave a small, scared smile and retreated. She almost scuttled backward.

The children followed and Giuseppe stood blocking the doorway, arms crossed, an islander in defence mode.

'Help,' Anna said to Leo, distressed beyond measure.

'It's okay,' he said, rising and coming to her aid. He put his arm around her waist, as protective a gesture as Giuseppe's. 'Don't take it personally. You are...'

'I know, a Castlavaran.' She sighed. 'Okay, Leo, I know I am. But I will make a difference. But twenty years... Wow, Leo...' And then she grimaced and pulled herself away from him.

'Please, Giuseppe, reassure Sofia that the last thing I want is to take her away from this *taverna*, from you and your children and this magic place. And you know the reason? I intend to come back here once a week for the next twenty years, maybe even more, and sit under your olive trees and eat your pasta and calamari. If that's okay with you.'

'You will come?' Giuseppe said cautiously. 'With Dr Aretino?'

'Mostly without,' Anna said, suddenly brisk. 'I intend to enjoy myself on this island, but it's starting to dawn on me... I may have to enjoy myself alone.'

She headed back to the table and sat and helped

herself to another tentacle. Firmly, as if the action was a vow.

Leo was left looking at Giuseppe. The older man stared at Anna and then shrugged. It's in the lap of the gods, his body language said, and Leo could only agree.

He managed a smile and turned back to watch the woman he'd once loved…

Still loved…

Twenty years?

It was, indeed, in the lap of the gods.

CHAPTER EIGHT

Six months later

SHE WAS ON the beach. It was nine at night. She'd spent the day immersed in plans, in building, in the general chaos of transforming an ancient castle into a modern medical facility. The noise of jackhammers, of carpenters, of architects talking at her, had given her a thumping headache.

This would be the architect ringing, she thought, or one of the builders. It seemed the entire island was determined to get this hospital up and running, and if it needed communication at midnight then so be it.

The last six months had passed in a whirlwind of activity. There'd been an intense meeting with the trustees in Milan, who'd turned out to be astonishingly enthusiastic.

'There's been little we could do from the sidelines over the years. But if you really do want to help Tovahna...'

She really did. They explained the legal intricacies and she'd struggled to understand, but she thought she had it sorted now.

She'd pensioned Victoir off. He might be repulsive but he'd kept her cousin and her uncle happy. In his place Martin had helped her appoint a good financial team. He and Jennifer had come and stayed for a week. Together they'd helped her understand the financial jargon and they'd helped her face down Victoir. There was something comforting about standing beside a competent lawyer. The alternative would have been to use Leo and she'd made a conscious decision to Not Need Leo.

Her dogs had arrived with Martin and Jennifer, and with them had come a sense of home. She'd explored the island with them. She'd met islander after islander. She'd tasted more homemade grappa and limoncello than was good for her. She hadn't quite dived into the dating scene—as if she could when every islander regarded her in awe—but she'd enjoyed herself.

She still felt an outsider but she'd accepted her lot. The islanders remained wary but she was doing things that made her happy.

And Leo? She scarcely saw him. He made time

to be at the planning meetings, but those meetings consisted of architects, hospital planners, builders, suppliers. As soon as they left, so did he.

He had pressures of his own, she knew. Carla told her his mother was fading, and the island's medical need was still oppressive. Until the castle hospital was up and running the trustees couldn't justify her employing medical staff, and she could hardly help herself when there was so much to do here. She was working desperately to get essentials sorted. Some of it was in place but not nearly enough.

And now…her phone was ringing. Drat. She was so over building details.

She was walking in the shallows, kicking up a spray of water with her bare toes, watching her dogs romp ahead of her. The night was almost moonless but at some stage the security-conscious Victoir had had floodlights installed, so the beach was an island of light, backdropped by the castle.

The phone rang out—and then started again.

She sighed and tugged her phone from her back pocket, holding it up so she could see the caller ID.

Leo.

Her heart gave a stupid, crazy lurch.

Oh, for heaven's sake, get a grip. It'd be about planning…something. She hit receive and put on her most efficient voice.

'Hold, will you, Leo? I need to call the dogs. Boris, Daisy, here, guys, home time.'

The dogs wheeled back to her, lanky springer spaniels, glorying in their evening run but equally delighted to be heading back to share their mistress's bed.

That bed was far too big.

Don't go there.

'What can I do for you, Leo?' She started up the steps of the sea wall, her dogs at her heels. She had her voice under control, nicely efficient.

'Anna, I need your help. Two fishing trawlers hit in the harbour mouth. Idiots running without lights. I'm guessing bulbs blown and they saved money by not replacing them, both banking on others to have lights. One of the fuel tanks exploded. Reports of multiple burns. I know your theatre's not ready but I know it's close. First report is six injured crew. I'm on board a boat now, heading out to meet them. Anna, our emergency room is tiny. We can't cope with more than two.

We need you as a doctor but we also need space. I haven't been in it for weeks but…hell, Anna, how close are you?'

Six months ago, when she'd returned from negotiating with the trustees, Leo had rejected her offer to help at the hospital. 'Anna, a new hospital is central to the well-being of the entire island. If you can bear being away from medicine for a few months…'

He was right, it had been sensible, so she'd spent six months tied up in bureaucracy. She'd seen not one patient.

But tonight Leo was asking for help.

And she could help.

'Everything's ready to go,' she told him, feeling the familiar surge of adrenalin that medical emergencies produced. 'The surroundings look like a bomb site, but our casualty section's pretty much ready to receive. Equipment's been arriving over the last couple of weeks. We can fit eight in our reception area.'

There was a pause as he took that in. She could hear the sounds of emergency through the phone. She could hear the engine of the boat he was on, the sound of the wind in the background, people shouting. This beach was around the headland from the harbour so she could see nothing, but she imagined him on the deck heading toward flames, gearing up for disaster.

She wanted to be with him. She wanted…

What she wanted was immaterial. It was what she could give that mattered. She thought of the cramped emergency room he usually worked in and she thought of multiple burn casualties. She thought of the alternative.

'You saw it two weeks ago when the painting was done,' she said. 'But we've gone further. When the equipment orders came through I decided it was dumb leaving it in storage until the whole project was completed. Everything's unpacked. I've had the place cleaned, sterilised. Two theatres are ready to go. I don't have drugs yet, but I imagine they'd be easy to transport from your hospital. I have eight cubicles ready.'

Burn victims needed to be treated fast. There'd be blistering, heat welding fingers to fingers or, worse, shock, hypothermia, heart failure. After severe burns these would be more than possibilities. Without swift, competent treatment, death was a probability, disfigurement certain. They'd need evacuation—no small hospital had the facilities to care for major burns victims long term—but initial stabilisation was imperative.

'You can bring them to the jetty under the castle wall,' she said while Leo thought through implications. 'Is Carla at the hospital?'

'Bruno's there, organising receiving. Carla and Freya are on their way in.'

'They could come straight here. How many inpatients do you have over there?'

'Seven but none risky.' There was another silence and she could almost hear the cogs working. 'I'll take you at your word, then. Eight reception cubicles. Surgical equipment?'

'Everything but drugs.'

And the decision was made. 'I've already put out a call for all available staff. I'll have Bruno redirect them to you. I'll leave one nurse at the hospital. It's a risk but a smaller one than trying to cram burns victims into a place geared for four at the most. Bruno can bring the drugs now.' She heard a shout in the background and then another, fainter, in response. 'I'll leave reception to you, Anna. We're reaching the scene now.'

'You don't want me to get on a boat and come out?'

'You're better there. We're only ten minutes

from the castle. The boats can bring them straight in. I'll do emergency resus, but everything else will be sent to you. Bless you.'

'Bless you back again,' she said, and she couldn't quite keep her voice steady. She was imagining two boats colliding in the dark, fire, spilled fuel, major injuries. As a family doctor she'd had no experience of the kind of accident Leo was facing. She had the training, though, and so did Leo.

They were both going to need it.

The scene facing Leo was appalling.

Debris was scattered on the water, pieces of still-burning timber. The boat was already a charred hull. The other was a wreck.

He knew these boats, and their crews. World Cup football was being screened tonight at the town hall. The skippers would have been trying to get into port before the game started.

Entering harbour without riding lights? What a way to save money.

The local *guardia* boat was already on scene, as were a couple of other boats, local fishermen who'd also have been on their way into harbour.

There were two dinghies on the water, being rowed. You didn't start a motor with this amount of spilled and burning fuel. He saw fishermen hauling someone aboard. A body? Any hope that the initial call might have overstated the seriousness of the situation disappeared.

'Doc…' Pietro, head of the island's *guardia*, called to him across the water. 'We have two on board here, in a mess. There are four on board the *Marika*, maybe less injured but I can't say for sure. Another's being pulled in now but it looks like we've lost him. One unaccounted for.'

'Send the *Marika* straight in,' he called. With patients on two boats he couldn't even assess in the time it'd take to them back to the castle. 'Take them to the castle jetty.'

'The castle…'

'Dr Raymond is waiting.'

'The *Castlavaran*?' Despite the urgency of the situation he heard disbelief. Angelo, the dour skipper of the *Marika*, was calling to him in incredulity. 'We need *you* to treat them. Or Carla. Why would we take them to the *castle*?'

There'd been disbelief at the concept of what Anna was doing. Islanders were taking wages for their work, as generations of Tovahnans had been taking wages, but there'd been little trust.

'It'll turn out to be just for the wealthy; just wait and see.'

Leo had heard the mutterings.

And here it was, suspicion loaded into the one word the skipper had called. He'd said *castle* like another might have said poison. 'We'll take them to the hospital, no?'

'No. The castle's set up for triage. You know we've been working to get it ready, and tonight we're using it. Bruno, Freya and Carla and our nurses are all there. Just go, Angelo.' One of the dinghies was alongside now and there was no time for more persuasion. 'Make sure every airway's clear and there's constant water running over burns. Go.'

And Angelo cast him a look of disbelief—but then moved to obey.

Trust, Leo thought. How hard it had been to earn and how important that he have it. The hatred of all things Castlavaran was bone deep in all islanders. They'd seen what Anna was doing. They'd heard of what she'd done to help save Carla, but centuries of mistrust couldn't end in months. They were all waiting for the drawbridge to slam down. For Anna to show her true colours.

But tonight he'd demanded trust and he had it. The *Marika* was heading for the castle, mistrust of Anna or not, and he had to focus on his own work.

The fisherman pulled from the water wasn't dead. Not quite. He'd swallowed water, however, lots of it, and had probably breathed in burning fumes. It took all Leo's skills to resuscitate him. He was sending him on to the castle on one of the fishing boats as he heard a hail from across the water.

'Doc, we've found Giulio. He was trying to swim to shore. He doesn't look good.'

That was an understatement. What came next was thirty minutes' intense, heartbreaking effort and at the end he lost.

What adrenalin charge had enabled a burned, shocked fisherman to try and swim to shore? Giulio was well into his seventies. He had a weakened heart already and he should have had a valve replacement years ago. *'But where's a man like me to find money for a stay in a foreign hospital? I won't put my family in debt. No, this old heart will give out when it decides.'*

It decided tonight.

The final boat took Leo to the castle jetty, with Giulio's body. He stood beside the shrouded stretcher and felt the weight of isolation, of poverty, of the responsibility of being a doctor in charge of a nightmare.

There'd been forerunners of nights like this on the island before, disasters with multiple casualties, and each had left him with the same sense of helplessness. His hospital wasn't geared to cope, and people had died because of it.

What was new? He'd felt helpless from the day his father had died, of appendicitis, of all things, an appendix ruptured because there'd been no doctor, no hospital. Twenty-four hours of agony.

He'd vowed that no one would die that way again. But now he was stuck on a boat and who knew what was happening in the castle? Bruno and Freya were young, inexperienced, full of good intentions but they should be supervised. Carla had come back to work after her illness but she lacked the decisiveness of the old Carla. Her hands shook a little. She faltered when there was no room for faltering.

Which left Anna.

The castle loomed above them as they neared the jetty. Its presence was vast, dark and forbidding.

What had he done, suggesting they use it? Would it create more confusion?

He was depending on Anna, depending on her promises, and he, of all people, should know that promises meant nothing.

Memories were suddenly, inappropriately, flooding back. One amazing night.

'We'll have children, practise medicine together, have an awesome life. Anna, will you marry me?'

And then that appalling dinner with her mother...handing back the ring and walking away.

Hell.

There were shouts from the jetty, torches beaming out over the water, guiding them in. Locals, who before Anna had arrived had never been permitted within the castle confines. She *was* making a difference.

He glanced down at the shrouded shape of what once had been Giulio. A life well lived, but a useless, stupid death.

That was how he felt right now. Useless. He'd

vowed to make a difference to this island but people were still dying.

People would still die and they'd die tonight. He'd seen enough of those who'd already been shifted to the castle. It'd take a miracle, and what Anna was providing...

It was no miracle. She was doing her best but the long legacy of the Castlavarans remained intact.

History couldn't be changed.

She couldn't help.

He was twenty-three years old and he was dying under her hands.

She had the emergency room set up just as she'd envisaged it. She had staff working as a team. They'd cooled every burn, at least twenty minutes under running water. They'd administered pain relief. They'd coped with immediate shock and blood loss, treating lacerations and breaks from the impact itself. They'd made sure, as much as possible, that pain levels were under control.

Bruno and Freya were wrapping burned limbs with plastic film, which protected as well as helped with pain. Carla was coping with a fractured arm that, if not splinted, could well block circulation.

She had no idea what Leo was facing. What he was coping with on his own.

But she had little time to think of Leo. She was adjusting the oxygen on the fisherman she was starting to think she'd lose.

His name was Tomas. Bruno had recognised him when they'd admitted him, though how anyone could recognise the blacked figure was beyond her.

'He's my kid brother's best mate,' Bruno had told her, visibly distressed. 'Anna, I can't...'

None of them could. Bruno and Freya were nurse-practitioners whose experience of severe burns was almost nil. Carla had treated burns, but since her stroke she'd become increasingly unsure.

Family medicine hadn't prepared Anna for this. She was upping oxygen, trying desperately to think what to do next, but there was no option in her grab-bag of emergency training. She was watching Tomas fighting for each breath, listening to the rasping in his chest, watching him almost visibly losing the fight.

And then Leo walked into the room and she could have wept with relief.

She'd glanced up as she heard one of the nurses greet him but almost immediately her attention went back to Tomas.

'What's happening?' Miraculously he was beside her. Directed by the nurse? Everyone in this room knew how tenuous was Tomas's hold on life.

'Leo.' Even saying his name stilled her panic. 'Tomas and I could use your advice.'

Heaven only knew the effort it cost to keep her voice calm. What she wanted was to scream for help, tell him she was out of her depth and drowning, but Tomas was still conscious. The last thing an injured patient needed was their doctor confessing she didn't have a clue what to do next.

'Tomas, Dr Aretino's here,' she told him, unsure what Tomas could or couldn't see through his swollen eyelids. 'I'll give him a quick summary of what's happened to you. Leo, Tomas has oropharyngeal and neck burns. I've intubated but he's still struggling. We've cooled and wrapped the burns. We've administered pain relief and fluids. I'd have expected the intubation to assist.'

She paused then, and said nothing more. The next word, the most logical word in her description was 'but'. *But nothing's helping.*

She didn't say it. Tomas didn't need to hear it, and to Leo it would be obvious.

She stepped back a little so Leo could see.

The nurses had helped her soak, strip and cut away Tomas's charred clothing. If she'd had to guess she'd say he'd borne the brunt of the explosion. His chest was a mess, with impact wounds as well as burns.

Intubation should have made a difference, but it hadn't brought the immediate relief she'd prayed for. There was reduced oxygen saturation, a delayed capillary refill. His chest was hardly moving—there was shallow respiratory effort and limited abdominal wall movement. It was as if he was so badly burned inside that nothing could work.

She watched Leo do a fast visual assessment and then she saw his hand close over Tomas's undamaged wrist.

'Tomas. You've got yourself in one hell of a mess,' he said. 'But, hey, you're the first patient to be treated in Dr Anna's Amazing Castle Hospital. How lucky are you? We have brand-new operating theatres, every state-of-the-art tool for any impressive piece of surgery we want to perform, and Anna and I are aching to try out our new toys. You're our guinea pig.'

It was a scary concept but Leo's voice was warm and strong and reassuring and Anna saw the tiny slump of relaxation, the lessening of the flight and fight reaction that told her Tomas trusted Leo.

Leo was known. He was an islander.

She'd never be that.

But this was hardly the time to think that. Leo was looking at her, signalling her with his eyes. To back him.

'Tomas, the plan is now to put you to sleep in one of Dr Anna's great new theatres,' he told him, but he was still watching Anna, sending a silent message to follow his lead. 'Something hot has banged hard into your chest. In the long run you'll have a really impressive scar to show your grandkids, but right now it's created a band of tissue that's injured and swelling. It's acting like a corset, restricting your chest and making breathing harder.

'You've seen those old movies where the lady faints because her corset's too tight? That's what's happening to you. What we need is to give you another neat scar while we loosen the restriction. It'll be like cutting the corset's laces. It's a quick procedure under anaesthesia so you won't feel a thing and it'll make your breathing a whole lot easier. Is that okay with you?'

Tomas hardly moved but his body seemed to slump. Letting go? Placing his fate into Leo's hands.

Which was pretty much how Anna was feeling. She was ceding to Leo.

She'd never seen anyone with this extent of burn and injury. What Leo was intending to do... The procedure was called escharotomy. She'd learned of it in her training—the slicing of injured flesh to relieve pressure—but she'd never performed it. And here was Leo, acting as if it was common-or-garden normal.

'Let's go, people,' Leo said quietly, as if there was no rush at all, but minutes later they were in Theatre. The Castle Hospital Theatre. Never used until now.

What good fairy had made her work herself almost to exhaustion to get this ready? Anna wondered. She'd checked and double-checked to have everything in readiness, even though she hadn't expected patients for weeks or even months. She'd paid for a surgical colleague to come from England and check it with her. The theatre was big, airy, superbly lit and right now it was fully staffed. Bruno had brought the drugs they needed, plus back-up equipment from the old hospital. Maria was acting as head theatre nurse and a younger nurse was working as her assistant.

Anna's role was to give the anaesthetic. That took all her skill and more, because giving anaesthetic to such a severely burned patient was way beyond her area of expertise.

Leo was operating as if this was entirely within his skill set.

He was also keeping a respectful eye on her.

'Is there anyone else who's more competent?' she'd whispered as they'd scrubbed, but he'd shaken his head.

'Carla's still unsteady. She knows her limits and she wants you to do it. You can do it, Anna.'

'Leo, with this amount of respiratory distress…'

'Just haul up everything you know and then some,' he told her. 'And if you want back-up, ask.'

'Ask you?'

'We've never had a qualified anaesthetist,' he told her. 'Carla and I have struggled through. We've read, teaching ourselves until we can spout oxygen saturation levels, respiratory flows in our sleep. But even before this last illness Carla's been slowing down, becoming unsure. Her arthritis has made her fingers stiff and it's knocked her confidence. I've been starting to share, backing her decisions at every turn. So if you have any questions, ask. I won't be judging.'

She wasn't considering his opinion of her. She wasn't beginning to think he was judging her. She knew he was simply grateful that he had a pair of hands with medical skill.

He'd do whatever it took to protect his islanders.

Hadn't she learned that the hard way?

There it was again, history, surfacing when she had no time to give it space and no inclination either. It had been with her for the full six months of her stay, in consultation meetings, when they were focussed on the complexities of getting this place up and running, when they were talking staffing, when he was striding through the building site, snapping questions... And now, when he was all doctor, with every fibre of his being focussed on keeping Tomas alive…

That was what she was, too, a doctor operating outside her skill range, dredging up every last thing she'd been taught in medical lectures so long ago.

And all the while she was conscious that this was Leo. Not just a colleague. *Leo.*

It was almost as if her body had an inbuilt warning sign and it was flashing red. Do not think about how much he cares for his people. Do not admire the skill of those amazing fingers, or admit that Leo is simply…

Someone she loved?

She shoved the thought away as she focussed on the dials that told her Tomas's heart continued to beat, his oxygen saturation was rising, he might just possibly make it.

Thanks to Leo. And Leo's decision to return here.

Which was why personal history had no place here.

Blessedly the technicalities of what she was trying to do took over. Leo was cutting through the constricting, charred outer layer of flesh. He worked with an assurance Anna could only wonder at, cutting skilfully along the mid-axillary line of the chest. There were so many constraints he had to be wary of. The last thing Tomas needed was more damage, but not for a moment did Leo act as if he was unsure.

And almost the moment the cut was made, Tomas's chest started falling and rising with less restriction, moving naturally as it needed to if Tomas was going to breathe on his own.

Finally Leo started cauterisation, sealing the wound to stop the bleeding. He was working swiftly, not with the painstaking care that he'd use if the scar he'd made would be the scar Tomas would carry for life. There'd be more scars on this chest, months if not years of treatment to get Tomas back to anywhere near normal. Skin graft after skin graft. An instant's carelessness in the harbour would be followed by years of regret.

Maybe everyone in the theatre was thinking that. The silence in the theatre was suddenly loaded.

'We need to leave him in an induced coma,' Leo said into the stillness. 'The brain needs to focus on healing rather than shock and pain. He'll be on the first transfer out.'

She nodded. She knew by now how much the

islanders hated leaving the island for treatment but with burns this severe there was little choice. They'd done all they could for Tomas. 'I'll stay with him,' she told Leo. 'You head back to the fray.' And then she hesitated. She'd heard reports of what had been happening out on the water. 'Giulio?'

'He died,' he said roughly, and she heard grief and exhaustion in his words. One of the nurses fought back a sob and Leo's face reflected it.

These were his people. His home.

'Any man's death diminishes me.' She used to think of the quote from John Donne when someone in her small English village died, someone she'd cared for, but she hadn't been born there, raised there. She hadn't gone to school with the locals, shared their backgrounds. She wasn't entitled to share their grief.

She watched as Leo's shoulders slumped as he told them of Giulio's death, and then she watched as he braced and headed back to treat whoever was left.

She felt for him.

And stupidly she felt bereft—for herself.

Tomas couldn't be left. He needed intense nursing and none of the nurses had the skills to care for him. She stayed in the now almost empty theatre and she watched as Tomas's chest rose and fell, rose and fell.

He'd live because of Leo.

There'd be no regrets this night, she decided, or none from her. The bigger picture was that Leo had come back to do what was right for his country. The bigger picture was that she could keep this medical centre growing, help Tovahna free itself from the shackles of poverty.

They were huge things, and they shouldn't leave one inch spare for the moments of emptiness that wouldn't go away.

CHAPTER NINE

THE LAST HELICOPTER left at dawn. There'd been three, all manned with medics trained in trauma medicine. Tomas had been evacuated first. The others had followed. Every one of them had suffered burns. Every one of them would need treatment by overseas specialists.

The choppers had used the castle roof to land. That had been another thing Anna had done over the months she'd been there, clearing debris, removing any impediment to a large chopper landing.

She should feel good that it had worked, she thought, as she watched the last chopper lift and head into the rising sun. Instead she felt empty. She was watching Leo. He'd done the handover to the chopper's medical staff. Now he stood back. His shoulders were slumped. He looked... gutted.

'They'll all make it.' She said it quietly, because his body language spoke of solitude and she wasn't sure she had the right to intrude. 'Even Tomas. His arms and legs are okay. His throat was swollen but his face doesn't seem too bad.' He must have fallen to his knees as the explosion hit, she thought, as the flames had formed a band of burned flesh around his chest. The rest of his wounds seemed relatively minor.

'But at what cost?' Leo was still staring at the disappearing chopper. 'Have you any idea…?' He broke off. 'Sorry. There's nothing you can do.'

'There might be,' she said diffidently.

'There isn't. You've done enough. That you had the castle ready…that was a miracle in itself. We can't hope for more.'

'Maybe,' she said, and let the word settle for a while. Let her thoughts settle.

There'd been time for thinking in the hours she'd sat by Tomas, listening to the noises from outside her new theatre, the sounds of a medical team working hard, the distant cries of distressed relatives. She'd have to prepare a reception area out of earshot of the emergency centre, she'd decided. She'd thought of that during the long hours and she'd thought of a lot more.

'I might need to talk to Victoir,' she said diffidently, and waited. She wasn't sure Leo was in the mood to listen to plans.

She wasn't sure of anything.

'Why would you talk to Victoir?' His voice was flat, disinterested. Defeated?

'Because he's dishonest.'

'Sorry?' He turned to face her then, looking confused. Good, she thought. Anything to shake him from his distress.

'You know Martin went through the books while he was here?' she said, still diffidently. 'Victoir's been lining his own pockets for years, in all sorts of constructive ways.'

'So what's that got to do with now?'

'Because it seems that two weeks from now I'm holding a celebration,' she told him. 'A party to end all parties, a day to mark the opening of the castle to the island.'

'What… A celebration?'

'You haven't heard about it yet? How odd.' She ventured a smile. 'Okay, the place isn't near finished but I'm impatient and I want a party now. So it seems I've been planning one for weeks. I may need to do a bit of sleight of hand in my diary. The trustees do need the letter of the law to be followed but they're not about to inspect too closely.'

'I don't get it.'

'But I do,' she told him, willing the grief and shock to fade from his face. 'We're having an Open Castle Party to show everyone what we're doing. Any islander wanting to come will be welcome. It'll be awesome, and of course we need food. Lots of food.'

'Anna, I hardly think—'

'That talking parties now is appropriate? It is,' she told him. 'It must be. Hear me out. Leo, you may not know it but my cousin and my uncle seem to have been paranoid about supply. There's room here to store enough food to feed an army. There's a massive stockroom under the castle. Right now it holds tins of baked beans that are fifty years out of date. So many tins. We have a bank of freezers with enough space to store food for the castle for a year or more, and they're currently unused.'

'Yes, but—'

'So tonight I've been trying to figure a way I can help the injured fishermen. Their treatment, their rehab will cost a fortune. The terms of the

Trust won't let me help, but if they were working for me...'

'They were fishing.'

'Exactly,' she said, and smiled again, pleased with the neat plan she'd devised. The night had been totally miserable until she'd found this sliver of an idea. 'So here's my plan, aided by the not-so-honest Victoir. There'll be a document discovered tomorrow, dated...a couple of days ago? I'll leave it to Victoir to figure the niceties. It seems two days ago I requested two Tovahnan boats to put to sea to catch sufficient fish to stock my freezers. There'll also be backdated requests for hiring chefs, and there'll be menus discovered that might just contain the fish destroyed in last night's accident.

'I agree, it's complex. It'll take a few people crossing their fingers behind their backs, and co-operation by the locals, but the bottom line will be that all those injured were employed by the castle. By me. For my personal pleasure. Therefore the Trust is responsible for all their ongoing medical care.'

There was a long silence. A stunned silence.

'Do you know how much we're talking?' Leo asked at last. 'Treatment by the best burns units.

Specialist care. Rehab. And then there's Giulio. He died, Anna. There's his funeral, plus he and his wife lived on the boat. If he was on your payroll...'

'Leo, can I get it into your head that I don't consider this place mine? The money doesn't seem mine either, and compared to what's in the bank this'll be peanuts. I can't see myself doing much more than dinting the capital, no matter how I try. But I have to try. My relatives bled this island dry to fill the castle coffers and it's not my money. It belongs to the islanders. So... Dr. Aretino, is it a good idea or is it not?'

He stared at her, stunned. 'It's a brilliant idea,' he admitted at last. 'If you really mean it.'

'Of course I mean it. Do you think the islanders will come to my party?'

'When it's explained what it's for...you won't keep them away.'

'Excellent.' She sighed and rolled her shoulders and thought of her bed. She was bone weary, but to go to bed now... She wouldn't sleep. And neither would Leo, she thought. She watched his face and saw her exhaustion reflected there. But she also saw more.

Her help was appreciated, but underlying everything was the fact that he'd lost an islander tonight. One of his own.

She glanced downward at the waves gently lapping the shore under the castle walls. The morning sun was just starting to create its early-morning sparkle.

She felt tired and dirty and dispirited, and Leo must be feeling the same, only so much more. Left to his own devices he'd head back to the other hospital.

There was nothing major there. The nurses could cope. He had his phone—they could ring if anything came up.

If he put the ringer on loud they could hear it over the water.

So why not?

'Leo, I'm going for a swim,' she threw at him. 'Want to come?'

'What, now?'

'You were heading for a shower, right? There's a freshwater shower down below. You can swim and shower and then you're on your way. Coming?'

He was torn. She could see it, but she wasn't about to push further.

'I'm heading down,' she told him. 'I even know

my own way now. Three sets of stairs from here, turn left, halfway along there's a wooden door with huge brass bars. Lift the bar and you're at the castle swimming pool—you know it's sea bath hewn from rock with a channel at the end to swim out to the sea if you want? I do want. I might not think of this castle as belonging to me, Leo Aretino, but right now I'm thinking of that pool as mine, all mine. So join me if you want, the choice is yours.' And she headed for the stairs and disappeared.

He should go home.

He should check on his mother and then head back to the hospital.

His aunt was with his mother—bless her. And the hospital...

He made two fast phone calls. He wasn't needed.

Still, he should go home. There were so many reasons he should try for a couple of hours' sleep before the next crisis.

He glanced at the steps. From down below he heard a splash.

He glanced over the parapet, half expecting Anna to be waving up at him. Instead he saw her head down, stroking purposefully toward the end of the pool.

Almost naked. She was wearing knickers, nothing else, and her lovely, lithe body was streaking through the water like an otter's, as if swimming was second nature. Where had she learned to swim like that? It was almost as if she was an islander.

She wasn't an islander, he reminded himself harshly.

He should go.

But the sight of her swimming through the clear, sapphire water…the shock of the night…exhaustion… His head wasn't working as it should.

He wanted a swim. More, he wanted a swim with Anna.

He swore softly to himself, torn between sense and desire.

He was too tired for sense to prevail. He was too shocked, too exhausted, too needful.

His body only wanted one thing and his head had no power to resist.

He wanted to be with Anna.

The water was a blessing. It had always been.

Her mother had swum as if she'd been born to

the water, and from the time she could remember swimming had been part of their lives. There'd been all sorts of complications in Katrina's life but when things had got truly bad somehow she'd end up at a beach or a lake or a swimming pool.

'You can forget when you swim,' she'd told her little daughter. 'Don't let yourself think how cold it is, or what you have waiting for you after. Let yourself be a sleek, shiny fish, and the water's all yours. It's your home, baby. It's your safe place.'

As she'd grown older, as she'd realised how few safe places Katrina had, Anna had learned to almost fear her mother's passion for swimming. She'd arrive at Anna's apartment totally out of control, after some disastrous love affair, or a drug bust, or some other catastrophe. 'Get me to a swimming pool, darling. Or, better, get me to the beach.'

There'd been midwinter swims at stony beaches. There'd been break-ins to local pools at midnight, and Anna had mostly gone along because she'd known that in the water her mother was at peace.

And now at the castle she knew why. Her mother's childhood had, by all accounts, been solitary and miserable, but in the water under the castle Anna had found a similar peace.

It wasn't cold here. There were no fences to break. The water practically welcomed you in. For the six months she'd been here she'd swum every day and, like her mother, the time in the water was her time out.

She'd left Leo on the parapet. She had no idea whether he'd join her but it almost didn't matter. She put her head down and swam.

And he did join her.

She was in the 'swimming pool', which was simply a hollow hewn out of rocks at the base of the castle. As long as an Olympic pool, its waters were constantly refreshed by the waters lapping over the edge at high tide. The base at the shallow end was sand. At the far end, sea grasses attached themselves to the rocky floor, and tiny fishes, safe in here from larger predators, darted among the fronds. Their bright colours glinted in the morning light.

Anna saw them as she passed, but her mind had gone into the almost meditative state that swimming induced in her.

But then Leo was swimming beside her and meditation went right out the window.

He was as strong a swimmer as she was. Maybe even stronger. She'd been swimming hard and fast, as she always did at first, until the troubles of the outside world subsided. There weren't many who could keep up with her but Leo did it easily. They swam stroke for stroke. Side by side.

There was no need for them to swim side by side. The pool was almost as wide as it was long, but she didn't move apart and neither did he.

He was wearing only boxers. His body was so close if she edged a couple of inches to her left she'd brush his chest.

Skin against skin.

She was wearing panties. Nothing else. Bras were useless when you swam, they didn't stretch enough, making her feel constricted. She could have headed back to her apartment and donned a swimsuit when she'd left Leo but the pool was hidden from view from the windows above, and all she'd wanted was to be in the water.

And now…their swimming was in such synchronisation it was as if they were almost one.

She knew every inch of this man. His body… oh, she remembered his body, but now he was ten years older. His frame was stronger, the delineation of muscles more striking. He was a gorgeous Apollo of a man.

She wanted his body against hers. She wanted to say, *Mine*.

She wanted *him*.

She couldn't have what she wanted. Hadn't she learned that the hard way? Ten years of making do.

She hadn't been miserable for those ten years. After the first few appalling months she'd set to and made the most of what she had. She'd built herself a great career. She'd had some very nice boyfriends.

She'd always felt that part of her had been ripped away.

He was still beside her and the tension was suddenly unbearable. Enough. She swerved and headed for the cut leading to the open sea.

The bay wasn't quite as private but it was close. This bay was protected by two headlands, both within the castle keep. Last night's permission for islanders to use the castle jetty had been a one-off. It was glorious, it was safe and it was hers.

That was a jarring thought. She wouldn't think

it and she desperately hoped that Leo wasn't thinking it.

Maybe he was still in the pool. She wasn't looking. This whole night had her so disconcerted that her mind couldn't get anything straight. There was only the water, deep and clear and beautiful.

Rocks jutted up to the left, tiny islands, their surfaces worn smooth by the wash of high tides—or by generations of Castlavarians using them to sunbathe. Had ancestors sunbaked?

Sunbathing was free, therefore her ancestors probably had, she decided, and the thought of the miserliness of generations of Castlavarans had her kicking with extra strength.

She was filled with strange sensations, formed from the dramas and pressures of the night, the skills she'd had to dredge up, the sadness, and now the fatigue, the drop in adrenalin. But overriding all was the thought that Leo was somewhere behind her.

In the same ocean.

In the same world.

Will you marry me? The words were suddenly resonating.

He'd asked that of her ten years ago and she'd

said yes. They said wedding vows were inviolate. Maybe, for her, engagement was the same. Maybe she'd felt part of this man for ever.

Which was nonsense. She kicked out again, heading across the bay, fast and hard, letting the water cool something heating inside. Something she couldn't put a name to.

There were fish swimming under her, seeming almost to use her surge of power to carry them along. That was what she started to focus on. She wasn't alone, she had fish.

And her dogs back at the castle.

She didn't need Leo.

She reached the final rock before the open ocean and surfaced—and Leo was just behind her.

He was very large and very male and very wet. His body was glistening in the morning sunlight. He reached her rock and held on.

Their bodies brushed, skin against skin.

She wanted her bra back on. It'd been dumb to swim without it.

Actually, she wanted more. What was she doing, swimming almost naked? It was as if she'd issued an invitation. She should head to shore, grab her clothes and run.

She couldn't. She was winded, or at least that was what she told herself.

She tugged herself up onto the rock and dripped and stayed completely still. And waited.

He pulled himself up and sat beside her.

'Impressive,' he said. 'Your swimming.'

'It's one of the few legacies of any value my mother left me.'

'Swimming—and a castle.'

'Is that of value?' she said, because suddenly it had to be said. 'When it's messed with my life?'

'How does it mess with your life?'

'Because it stopped the man I love from wanting me.'

And there it was, out in the open. Said.

'Anna...'

'Just shut up,' she said, because she couldn't bear it one moment longer. He was too wet, too gorgeous, too close.

He was too Leo.

'Can we not talk?' she asked. 'Just...for now? I don't know about you but this time, this moment... I'm done. Right now I have only one need in the world and that need is you. Kiss me, Leo, before I go out of my mind.'

* * *

Of course he kissed her. How could he not?

She was simply the most beautiful woman he'd ever met, inside and out. She was naked apart from a sliver of lace panties. Her gorgeous, burnt-red curls were wisping wetly around her face. Her nose still had just the right number of freckles. Her body was brushing his, every curve just right.

Her lovely green eyes were gazing at him with what was surely a challenge.

Kiss me, Leo, before I go out of my mind.

Ditto, he thought. How can I not kiss her?

And he did.

She belonged to him, as simple as that. She'd made a vow ten years ago and that vow was as strong now as it had been then. Every nerve in her body confirmed it for her. She'd given her heart to this man and it still belonged to him.

He was hers.

It wasn't even a vow, she thought. It was simply a fact, a knowledge so deep and so strong that nothing could change it.

She shouldn't be out here. She shouldn't be

almost naked, kissing a man she'd had nothing to do with for ten long years.

But her body said it was right. Her hands held the wetness of his body against hers, she felt her breasts mould against his chest and she felt like…she'd come home.

This man. This body.

Hers.

His hands were holding her, claiming her, pulling her closer. His mouth was possessing hers, her passion answered by his and more. The warmth of him, the heat, the strength… This was right. This was where she wanted to be.

Her man.

He couldn't do this.

He was doing it. He was loving the woman he wanted with all his heart. But deep within, the ingrained learning was still there, and almost the moment he felt her body mould to his, the age-old lessons resurfaced. Like a ghost, taunting him from the past, refusing to be exorcised.

She was a Castlavaran.

Even as he took her into his arms, even as he succumbed to pure desire, the events of the night were still with him. The distrust of the men on the water. His demand that they trust.

They didn't trust Anna. Why should they?

They trusted him.

He was hers—and then he wasn't. She felt the moment he realised, the moment passion turned into something akin to despair. He pulled away and held her at arm's length, and it was all she could do not to sob.

'Anna, I can't,' he said, and his voice was ragged with emotion. She could almost see the war raging within. 'Not… I can't.'

'Why not?' Somehow she made her voice even. Somehow she stopped herself reaching out again.

But the world was moving in. She thought suddenly, stupidly, that the workers would be arriving at the castle soon. The new hospital wing was on the sea side, and windows were being installed. There'd be workers at those windows, and she and Leo were far enough away from the sheltering castle wall for them to be seen.

She raised her arms to her chest almost as a gesture of defence. Leo saw and grimaced.

'We need to get back. Are you right to swim?'

'Of course I'm right to swim.' It was almost a snap. 'But, Leo, about us…'

'There's no us.'

'Are you kidding? After this? You want me as much as I want you.' What was happening? She was so confused.

But the time for silence was over, she thought. They'd lost ten years. What did she have to lose by breaking the barrier of emptiness?

'Leo, ten years ago you walked away from me.' She was inordinately proud of how steady her voice sounded. 'I told myself that it was a teenage romance, nothing more. I moved on. Sort of. But now…the way I feel… The way you feel… Leo, this thing between us, it's real and it's strong. Can we continue to ignore it?'

'I think we must.'

'So tell me the reason,' she said, struggling to keep her voice even. 'You walked away from me. It seemed then that you betrayed me, you broke a promise, you broke my trust. But ten years later I still want you. More, I still need you.'

How much pride did she have to lose by saying that? she wondered, but she'd been six months in this place. Six months of knowing there was no other woman in Leo's life. Six months of knowing how much he loved his country, how strong his reasons had been for walking away.

'Leo, I believe I can trust again,' she said, and there was a wobble in her voice now that she couldn't disguise. She was laying so much on the line here. 'But can you?'

'I never stop trusting.'

'That's not true and you know it. You classified me as a Castlavaran and trust flew out the window.'

'It's not you,' he said, heavily now. 'But, yes, it's the Castlavaran thing. How can I go there?'

'You hardly have to go there,' she said with irony. 'In case you haven't noticed, you're sitting on a rock in the middle of the sea with an almost naked woman right by your side. This is not a large rock. Go there? I believe you're already there.'

'I shouldn't be.'

'So tell me why not? You don't love me?'

'Love's got nothing to do with it.'

'Really?' Anger was rising now. She was baring everything, her body and now her thoughts, laying everything on the line. But the look on his face... *He was about to say no?*

And here it came.

'Anna, do you know what you're asking of me?'

'What? It seems to me that I'm giving.'

'You are,' he said heavily. 'But that's part of the problem. Anna, we're poles apart and you need to accept that, because it's reality. I'm the son of an impoverished widow, and my father died because of the power imbalance, the money imbalance on this island. I've seen what power can do, and so have each and every one of these islanders.'

'It can change. It has changed and you know it.' The knot of anger, of resentment was growing stronger. She'd exposed herself so much, and here he was still classifying her. Just another Castlavaran. Just another power wielder.

'You need to think this through,' he said, urgently now. 'Let me paint the whole picture.'

'You need to.' She was shivering, despite the growing warmth of the sun. Rejection was all around her.

But Leo's face was resolute. Implacable. She thought suddenly of the expression she'd seen on his face all those years ago and she thought, Nothing's changed.

'Anna, what would the islanders think if we married?' He closed his eyes for a moment as if reinforcing his own thoughts, and when he opened them again she saw resolution in spades. 'They're cautiously optimistic about what you're doing now. Of course they are, but what you expect of them is trust and you can't buy that with six months of building. It takes generations to build it. And, Anna, they trust me.'

'Why wouldn't they?'

'There's any number of reasons they wouldn't. Anna, they allow me to vaccinate their children, and if you knew how long it took me to get them to agree… There's little internet access on the island—there's no infrastructure and no one can afford satellites. Poverty breeds superstition and fear. Carla hasn't been able to persuade them in all her years of practising medicine. You know why? Because the sister of her great-aunt by marriage was your grandfather's wife. That's how she got the money to pay for her medical training. She came back here and the islanders were grateful for her skills but they still didn't trust her. She could treat the worst of cases but she couldn't change things.'

It was her time to close her eyes then. She felt so bleak she was almost ill.

'So I'm a Castlavaran and I'm tainted.'

'By association, yes. No matter what I want... Anna, I can't risk it. I can't risk what I've built.'

'So after ten years nothing has changed.'

'It can't.' There was despair in his voice but she couldn't listen to his despair. It was nothing, she thought, compared to how she was feeling. Exposed. Betrayed. Helpless. All from a finger of fate she'd had nothing to do with.

'So that's that, then,' she said bleakly. 'We all live ever after, but happily doesn't come into it.'

'Anna, maybe you could—'

'Don't you dare,' she hissed, cutting over whatever he'd been about to say. There was nothing that could make this better. 'Don't even think about making suggestions as to what I could do or not do with my life. It has nothing to do with you. I'll get on with making this castle the best hospital I possibly can. I'll put every ounce of energy into making this island more liveable, making up as much as I can for the greed and selfishness of people I don't even consider my ancestors.

'But it seems I'm not allowed to love you. So I can't listen to what you think I should do personally. You butted out of my life ten years ago and obviously that decision sticks. Okay, I accept it. I've humiliated myself enough. From now on, you're my professional colleague and nothing more. So if you'll excuse me I need to get back to shore and get some clothes on. You set your barriers in place ten years ago and it's time I set mine up, just as rigidly.'

There was nothing left to say. She could feel tears slipping helplessly down her face.

He raised a hand as if to wipe them away, and she slapped it away.

'Don't touch me,' she managed. 'Not now and not ever.'

And she turned and dived into the water. She swam back to shore, hard and fast.

Sobbing underwater was hard, but she managed it.

She had the rest of her life to manage everything else.

Ten years ago Leo Aretino had walked away from the woman he loved because of loyalty to his country. He'd thought then that nothing could hurt more.

He'd been wrong. He sat and watched her swim away and the pain he felt was bone deep.

Ten years ago he'd argued that his cause was

noble. He'd thought separation would cause Anna pain but she'd get over it. She'd been young, beautiful, talented. Her life was in England. Walking away from her had felt like he was cutting away a part of himself, but he'd been young, he'd been optimistic and he'd been sure that Anna's pain on rejection would be fleeting.

Now, watching her swim away, having her words replay over and over in his head, that surety was gone.

He'd hurt her as badly as he'd hurt himself and that pain was ongoing.

So swim after her. Gather her into his arms. Be damned to the consequences, you love her.

But marriage to a Castlavaran…

The impossibility was still there.

Things were changing, he thought. Anna was building a medical service that could finally equal that of its neighbouring countries. She was building not only a hospital but also apartments luxurious enough to attract medical staff. The castle would be transformed into a hospital that the islanders trusted and used.

But he had no doubt that tonight the boats had brought the injured to the castle because of him. Trust in him had allowed burned men to be brought into a medical centre that seemed almost foreign. More. Foreign didn't begin to describe the islanders' distrust of all things Castlavaran.

If he was seen to align himself with Anna… If he was to become part of the Castlavaran family…

Maybe it could work. Given time.

But if it didn't… If the islanders didn't accept assurances…

He thought of the fledgling vaccination programme that he'd worked so hard to get off the ground. He thought of the home rehab programmes he'd set up for so many people. He thought of diet charts, diabetic schedules, exercise regimes. He thought of child and adolescent health programmes he'd instigated. They all sounded simple, sensible, but for an island cut off by poverty for so long, they were huge.

They existed because he was seen as one of them. He was an islander the people themselves had sent away to train. He knew he was trusted.

He wasn't a Castlavaran.

Anna had reached the beach now. He saw her grab her clothes, slip a T-shirt over her head and start to make her way up the ancient steps, to disappear into the castle. To her fantastical apartments.

To where she belonged. To where fate had decreed she stay.

Whereas he belonged elsewhere. Not in her castle. Not even on this rock, or on this beach, which had been controlled for so long by a family who ruled by greed.

The weariness and grief he felt was making him feel ill, but part of that—a huge part—was grief for Anna. This morning he'd seen just how much he'd hurt her, but there was no escaping that hurt.

He was an Aretino, an islander. Anna was a Castlavaran. The middle ground was this magnificent new medical centre. Maybe it would work, because of Anna's generosity and because of the trust the islanders had in him and his staff, but that middle ground had to stay purely medical. The risks of muddying it were far, far too great.

Anna was gone. The castle loomed grey and forbidding and Anna was inside.

He had work to do. He needed to check on his mother. He had house-calls to make. He had a clinic to run.

Life went on. It had to.

And the love between two people? Like Romeo and Juliet, he thought suddenly, and found himself choking on a bitter laugh. Yeah, those two had sorted it well.

He'd always thought the story was ridiculous. Dying for a teenaged love? How stupid. They'd been kids. Given parental approval, given permission to see each other whenever they wanted, would they have been doing anything in their old age besides remembering with vague fondness—or even a bit of embarrassment—their first delicious romance?

Now he wasn't so sure—but he was sure that Romeo and Juliet had only thought of themselves and their grief. If Romeo had had the same level of duty and care as he did, could the Shakespearean ending have been the same?

That was crazy thinking, but at its heart he knew there was a germ of truth.

Given thought, care, the faith and dependence of his people, surely Romeo would have walked away.

Like Leo, he'd have had no choice.

CHAPTER TEN

THE CELEBRATION TWO weeks later, ostensibly to open the Castle Castlavaran Medical Centre, was definitely premature. The castle wasn't nearly ready but if Anna was to provide for the injured fishermen then the celebration had to be now.

'It's the opening of my special project,' she'd told the trustees in what was beginning to be a ritual contact rather than serious negotiation. 'You've let me build my hospital because I can't be happy practising my medicine without facilities to match. Now that the first section is open for emergency use, I need a party to celebrate.'

So the Deed of Trust, written so long ago, was invoked yet again. 'Funds shall be used for the pleasure of the present incumbent.'

Now, on the Saturday of what was to be a weekend of celebration, what she should be feeling was pleasure. She wasn't. Her morning's swim with Leo had pretty much destroyed her hard-won equilibrium, and she was back to being that dumb nineteen-year-old, in love all over again.

Which was dumb. What had changed? She still had her gorgeous apartments. She had her doofus dogs. She had her glorious beach. She had a project that took every waking hour, and she had an island home that'd make most millionaires swoon with envy.

She'd also had so little sleep she was running on empty and she was…desolate. That one kiss had thrown her straight back to feeling as if wedding vows had been broken.

But she couldn't think of that today. As the islanders streamed into the castle on this bright May Saturday, Anna walked slowly through the grounds, trying to see it through fresh eyes.

For the last couple of weeks she'd thrown everything into setting this place up so the islanders could see it as it would be. The plan was the Open Castle today followed by speeches and a feast, then a blessing by the local priest on Sunday morning. The whole weekend was designed to draw the locals in, make them see what she was doing—engender trust?

So now she did her own wandering through, trying to see it as the islanders were seeing it.

Outside areas first. The castle courtyard was to be separated into two. Right now it was filled with marquees, stalls providing food and drink, with hoopla stalls and fortune tellers—'Because an island party's not a party without them,' she'd told the trustees. But eventually—soon—it would be transformed, with an ambulance bay and reception area on one side, and a walled garden for ambulant patients on the other.

There were eventual plans to incorporate a visitors' precinct, art centre, tourist hub, formal tours of the underground labyrinth, history tours. For the hospital itself... She wanted a swimming pool, a rehabilitation centre to make major city hospitals weep in envy. Huge posters showed visitors her vision.

And now... The islanders certainly seemed happy—maybe they were—but everywhere she went, the moment she was seen, the noise level dropped to wary. She was greeted with politeness, with gratitude for what she was doing— but with distance.

She made her way up to the battlements, to the area that was to be converted to a massive patient lounge. This would be able to be cleared fast, at need, to be used as a helipad for patient evacuation, but there'd be covered areas with lounges, everything necessary for recovering patients to enjoy the sun and a view that up until now only Castlavarans had had the right to see.

There were more islanders here, showing huge interest as they inspected more posters showing plans. But there was still caution as Anna approached. She could still see distrust. What she gave, couldn't she take away?

She left the battlements and made her way down through what was still a rabbit warren of unused rooms, but with more posters showing them as individually designed wards, scrubbed, painted, hung with colourful curtains, with patchwork coverlets on the beds. Every detail had been meticulously thought out. There'd be work here for every islander who could sew. Yes, plain would be easier and even more hygienic, but this way there'd be wages coming into families who'd never seen such largesse.

'Pretty makes me happy,' she'd told the trustees, and, bemused, they'd simply signed off.

It did make her happy. Sort of. People were thanking her—awkwardly—but then turning back to their friends. To people they knew and trusted.

She walked into the last ward, the kids' ward. This had been a fun project and she'd started it early, so it didn't need posters to show what she intended. What had been the castle ballroom was now set up with cubicles, where removal of screens meant each child could become part of a communal recovery area.

She'd brought in occupational therapists to advise. The play area was designed for subtle rehabilitation, but it was fun and fantastical. It made her happy to see it.

But now she walked into the room and the customary silence fell. A group of locals admiring posters showing proposed play equipment parted to let her through.

Leo was at its centre.

Of course he was at its centre. He was part of this cautious, distrustful crowd. Part of the island.

During every step this last six months he'd talked to the islanders, told them what was happening, helped them to accept that there was no hidden agenda, no trap.

The islanders trusted him. If this was a democracy he'd be their elected president, she thought.

And Anna? She'd be the Crown. A figurehead,

to be accorded respect but not friendship. There was far too much history for a Castlavaran to be a friend.

There was too much history between herself and Leo.

'Dr Raymond.' He greeted her with a smile, though the smile didn't reach his eyes. 'This is wonderful.'

'I know,' she said, and gave him the same forced smile back. 'We should all be proud of what we've achieved.'

'*You've* achieved,' he said, raising his voice so all the islanders could hear. 'You're giving us generosity without price. And what you're doing for our injured fishermen… Believe me, we're grateful.'

There was a murmur of agreement. The islanders were indeed grateful, but she glanced around and she still saw wariness. The history of her ancestors was still there, an almost tangible thing, a history of abuse for financial gain. But in what way could she possibly gain by this, she thought, except the satisfaction of seeing an island cared for?

'Believe it or not, I don't want gratitude,' she managed—but suddenly she was caught.

Leo.

She looked at him, really looked at him. She'd thought he'd been laughing as she'd entered. Maybe he had, but there was no laughter here. He looked exhausted. It wasn't unusual to see Leo look tired, but this was different. His fatigue seemed bone deep.

'Leo, what's wrong?' She said it before she could help herself, but he shook his head, as if to tell her not to go there.

Well, why should she? They had no choice but to be nothing to each other. She shouldn't care that he looked as if he was driving himself into the ground.

The islanders were being polite. Smiling warily at her. They were assuring her how much they appreciated what she was doing. The thanks were effusive and she thought, They still think I can snatch it away.

But Leo… What was with him? Why the bleak look?

She couldn't care. He didn't want her to care.

It was almost time for the formalities. She'd organised for the head of trustees to formally open the emergency department—that seemed as close a gesture as she could make to declaring it was being handed over to the people. Then she'd asked Leo to speak and he'd reluctantly agreed.

'It's not my place,' he'd said, and she'd almost lost it.

'It's your island,' she'd told him. 'This is for your people. Just do it.'

So he'd agreed.

There'd be feasting and fireworks on the battlements. There'd be a blessing in the island church in the morning and then life would move on.

For twenty years.

But Leo didn't play his part.

The head of trustees gave a wonderful, generous introduction but Leo wasn't there to take over. It was Carla who finally rose to take his place.

'He must have been called away,' she told the crowd. 'But Dr Raymond is already trying to organise additional medical staff for us, so our Dr Leo might be able to have a well-deserved rest.'

She spoke warmly and well, but the gap left by Leo was almost palpable.

Still, it was a party. The fireworks were spectacular. The music was brilliant.

Anna still felt empty.

The silence as she approached, the forced way people responded to her, the wariness... When would it end?

In twenty years?

And then Carla found her. She was flushed, big-eyed, obviously worried. 'Anna, can you help?'

'Of course.' She'd been wondering how soon she could escape. She wouldn't mind a bit of medical need to give her an excuse.

'I think Leo's mother's dying,' Carla said, and Anna's heart sank. This wasn't the kind of medical need she'd had in mind.

'She's slipped badly over the last week and we're not sure how close the end is,' Carla told her. 'I'm guessing...close. Her sister—Leo's aunt—is starting to be frightened, so Leo's been sitting up with her these last few nights. But now he's tired to the point of collapse. We've had medical dramas this week, plus more than our share of births, and I know he's exhausted. He won't hear of me helping and all his relatives are here. He wants them to stay, to be part of the celebrations, but he's there alone. Anna, he's past exhaustion. If you're not needed here any more...would you go?'

'I'd go if I could be any use,' she said, puzzled. 'Carla, I'm not sure he'd want me.'

That was a heavy statement, but she knew it was true.

But now Carla was almost waspish, weariness and anger showing through her request for Anna to help. 'Of course he wants you,' she snapped. 'I know there are things between you—I'd be blind not to see it—but tonight he needs help, medical as well as personal. You need to get over yourselves, the pair of you, but meanwhile I need you... Donna needs you...to get over there. Here's the address. Can I depend on you?'

And there was nothing to say to that except, 'Of course.'

His mother was deeply asleep. There was time— even a need—to think of the events of the day.

The opening of this first step of the medical centre had been amazing. The plan was the culmination of everything he'd dreamed of for the island. It'd take a while to build a medical team with the skills to take advantage of the facilities Anna was providing, but already international interest within medical circles had been piqued. Doctors' quarters in a magnificent renovated castle would be a distinct lure, as was building a medical service almost from the ground up.

Island infrastructure was still a problem but Anna was already onto that. He'd heard her tell the head of the trustees…

'How can I be happy living here if I can't phone my friends on the other side of the island?'

There were so many issues facing the island, lack of good schools, good roads, a decent port, but Anna was onto those, too. He knew she'd find a way.

She was astounding.

She was the woman of his dreams and he couldn't claim her.

Maybe in three or four years when the medical team had settled, when the islanders had finally started to trust…

Or maybe not. How deep did mistrust of the Castlavarans go? For him to ally himself with a family that had essentially killed his father…

It couldn't happen.

He closed his mind, as he'd learned to do so often in the past when things hurt to the point where his chest felt as if it'd burst. As his chest felt like it was bursting now. His mother was slipping quietly from this life. She might rally, as she'd rallied before, but he knew the end was growing closer.

As a doctor he knew that this was a time for acceptance, but this was his mother. For so many years there'd been just the two of them. His distress was for memories of what had been. It was also fatigue—and for a build-up of emotion he could no longer hold back.

In the distance he could still hear the celebrations from the castle. He wasn't a part of them. They belonged…to the woman he loved?

He'd never felt so alone in his life.

Talk about the worst house in the best street! Realtors often said these were the best buys, but there was nothing 'best' about the house Carla had directed her to. The stone terraces here were crumbling, the façades sagging with time. The ground here must have shifted, maybe with some long-ago earth tremor, Anna thought, as the walls on each seemed out of alignment, plugged with timber, all slightly askew.

Leo's house was at the end of the row and its skew was the worst. Its woodwork was brightly painted. Its tiny front garden was a tangle of gorgeous vines and flowers—someone here had loved gardening—but nothing could disguise the meanness of its narrow façade, and the way it sagged toward the cobbled waterway at the end of the street.

Had Leo been paid nothing for the work he'd put into this island? For the local doctor to live in such a place...

But she wasn't here to judge. She knocked tentatively on the door. There was no answer. She pushed and the door swung open onto a small sitting room.

'Leo?'

'Anna!' She heard his shock. She pushed open the next door and Leo was inside.

As a doctor it was a scene she was familiar with. Acceptance came with experience of situations like this.

One look at Donna told her that the end, indeed, was close. She was a tiny woman and disease had shrunk her even more. The mass of white curls around her face was practically the sum of her. She lay completely still, and Anna wondered if this was sleep or coma.

'Carla said you might need me,' she said softly.

The shock was still with him. His hand was

holding his mother's and he didn't rise. 'Carla had no right.'

'Carla loves you—as all the islanders love you.'

There was silence at that. He turned back to look down into his mother's face and his distress was almost palpable.

'Unconscious?'

'She stirred a little while back. She asked for water.'

'She's asleep, then,' she said softly. 'Leo, when did *you* last sleep?'

'I can't remember.'

She nodded and walked across to lift Donna's emaciated wrist away from Leo. The pulse was steady. There was time yet, but who knew how long?

She put the old lady's hand back into his.

'You'll collapse if you don't sleep.'

'My aunt…she's the only one my mother trusts and she won't stay any more. She's scared.'

That happened. Death could be terrifying—or it could be a gentle slipping away, the culmination of a life well lived.

'Would you sleep for a couple of hours if I stayed with her?' she ventured. 'She doesn't know me but…'

'Of course she knows you. You're the Castla-varan.' It was said with something akin to desperation.

Now wasn't the time to argue. Anna simply nodded.

'If she knows that, then she'll also know I'm a doctor. She shouldn't be frightened if she stirs. But if she does stir and worries, Leo, I'll wake you straight away. I promise. Will you trust me that much?'

'You know I'd trust you…with everything I have.'

It was a big statement but she had to move past it.

'Then trust me with your mother,' she said. 'Let me take the chair. You go and find your bed and sleep.'

'Anna…after all I've done to you…'

'Don't go there,' she said softly. 'For now there's only your mother to think of, and your need for sleep.' He rose, and before she could help herself she laid her palm on his cheek. It was a caress of comfort, nothing more, and it seemed to ground them both.

'Sleep, Leo,' she said softly. 'I will wake you

the moment you're needed. Know that you can trust me.'

'I do trust you,' he said, and his voice was ragged with fatigue. 'Of course I trust you. But the whole island—'

'Forget about it,' she told him. 'Just go.'

And with one last long look at his mother—and then her—he went.

In the end it was a time of peace, sitting in the dark, listening to the thready breathing of the sleeping Donna. Maybe she should be distressed. Maybe the events of the day should have left her disoriented. But there was something about this time, this night, that said her world was some-how settling.

She was a stranger to this woman but she didn't feel like a stranger. This felt like her place.

She sat and let the stillness of the night envelop her and the rest of the world seemed to fade to nothing.

She should be tired but she didn't feel it. As the night wore on there was nothing but the sound of breathing. The sounds of peace.

And then, just before the dawn, Donna woke. Her dark eyes flickered open, focussing. The nightlight illuminated both their faces, but not so much. Enough.

'You…' It was the faintest of whispers. 'It *is* you. The Castlavaran.'

'I'm Anna,' she said softly. 'Leo's sleeping in the next room. Yes, I'm the Castlavaran.' What was the use of denying it now?

'You're the woman my son loves.'

There was no answer to that. She took Donna's hand to tuck it under the cover but it was grasped and held.

'I'll get Leo for you,' she told her. 'I'm sorry that you had to find me here, but you know I'm a doctor? Leo needed to sleep.'

'Don't be sorry. I'm sorry. You're Anna.' She sighed, a huge, regret-filled sigh of sorrow. 'Anna, he loves you.'

'And he can't marry me.' Why not say it like it was? 'Donna, it's okay. Your son won't do anything to put his family, or the islanders, at risk.'

'I know that,' Donna said distressfully, obviously making an Herculean effort to speak. 'But he fell in love. He has a photograph of you on his bedside table. He sent it to me all those years ago— "This is the woman I'm going to marry." And then nothing. Finally he explained and I agreed. Impossible. But I thought… I thought he must get over it. Move on.'

'That was…sensible.'

'It was selfish,' Donna told her, fighting for each word. 'Did he tell you? How could you ever know…?'

'Donna…'

'Let me say it.' The grip on her hand tightened. 'You know the Castlavarans killed his father? The night my husband came down with appendicitis… Carla was here then, our first ever doctor. She said the appendix had burst, that he needed emergency surgery and she couldn't do it here. I sent Leo to the castle to plead. He was twelve years old and we thought—it was the only way—a child pleading might just break down the Castlavaran indifference. We needed money to hire a helicopter. He wouldn't survive a boat trip to where he could get help. But your grandfather asked what was in it for him and then he slammed the door in Leo's face.'

'Oh, Donna…'

'And the stories go on,' Donna whispered, obviously fighting for breath to speak each word. 'Every islander has a story. So now… Anna, if there was any way he could do the work he needs to do with you by his side… If there was any way I thought he wouldn't lose the islanders' trust… What you're doing at the castle… I'm so proud of you. If I could see a way…'

'It's not for you to see our way for us,' Anna told her, wiping a tear slipping down the old lady's cheek. 'Leo and I will sort it out. We must.'

'He can't. He's like his father. He's too honourable…'

'I know that.'

'You'll have to do something,' Donna murmured. 'Please.'

'I'll do what I can.' She leaned over and kissed her lightly on her wrinkled cheek. 'Meanwhile, I promised I'd wake Leo the moment you woke and I'm honourable, too. Believe it or not.'

'I do,' Donna muttered fretfully. 'But can the islanders?'

He was soundly asleep, and it almost broke her to wake him. For a moment she stood, watching the steady fall and rise of his chest. He was still fully dressed, sleeping on top of the bed rather than in it. A big man in a small room.

She needed to call his name. He'd be awake in an instant, she thought. She'd promised to call.

But she took a moment, a moment only, to look around her.

The room was sparsely furnished. It was the room of a man who spent hardly any time here. There were faded marks on the walls, she guessed from childhood, from posters finally fallen down from where they'd been stuck on ancient plaster. The rugs were threadbare and the iron bedstead minimalist.

A decent sound system sat on the bedside table with good-quality headphones and she thought, At least he hasn't deprived himself of everything.

And then she saw the photograph.

It was small, black and white, enclosed in a simple silver frame.

She remembered when it had been taken. They'd just passed their exams and had gone to a fun fair. There'd been a photo booth and, laughing, sticky with fairy floss, they'd entered.

The picture was of two faces laughing from behind their mass of cotton candy. They were squashed so tightly together they almost seemed an extension of each other. It had been blown up from passport-sized and had been grainy, low-resolution in the first place, but their love and laughter showed through.

She had the matching print tucked in a bottom drawer. After all these years it hurt too much to see it, but that neither of them had destroyed it... Maybe such a thing couldn't be destroyed.

'If I could see a way...' Donna's words were still reverberating.

What way?

But she'd told Donna that now wasn't the time and she was right. She'd made a promise.

She leaned over and touched Leo on the shoulder. He was awake in an instant.

'She's okay, Leo. She's awake and talking.' It was all she could say. It wasn't for her to say what he knew for himself, that things were shutting down. 'She's just woken up.'

'I'll go to her.'

He rose and raked his hair.

And suddenly she was seeing him the night his father had died. Maybe he'd been woken from this bed, in this room. She thought of a twelve-year-old, woken from sleep, walking across the darkened drawbridge to the great castle gates. What a thing to ask of a child. How alone must he have felt?

He was alone now, facing the death of his

mother. Plus he was facing the ongoing needs this island had heaped on his shoulders.

She could help. She could share.

But for an Aretino to become a Castlavaran…

'If I could see a way…'

This island was so rigid but it had become this way through need—she'd accepted that. The castle and its owners were simply 'the Other'. You were an islander or a Castlavaran, not both.

If things could change…

They could change. With transfer of titles, with release of castle funds…

In twenty years.

It has to be possible, Anna thought. Her pride, her anger for the way she'd been treated had ebbed away. There was only aching need for this solitary man who'd done all in his power to make things good for his people.

He should be the Castlavaran, she thought. The ruler. He'd earned the right of respect, trust, the things a ruler needed. It shouldn't be her making these decisions. A tweak of fate had left the island in her hands but this man had earned it.

He stood, looking helplessly at her. His hand reached out for her—and then fell away uselessly.

'Anna, thank you. I'm sorry. I need to... You need...'

'We both need,' she told him, and something seemed to settle. Something solid. Something sure. He'd do what he had to do, this man. He was honourable. Dependable.

He was loved.

'Go to your mother,' she said softly. 'It's her need that has to take precedence now—but know that I go with you.'

And before she realised what she intended herself, she reached up and kissed him lightly on the lips. It was a feather touch, no more, a kiss given before he could react or reject, and then she was stepping away. 'Do what you need to do, Leo,' she said, and amazingly her voice even sounded sure. 'But go with my love. And know that I'm here for you and I will be here for you. For however long it takes.'

CHAPTER ELEVEN

THE FINAL PART of the opening of the medical centre took place the next morning. Anna had told the trustees that she needed a party, and Carla had set her straight on what else was needed.

'You're opening a medical centre and you want island acceptance? A blessing is non-negotiable.'

So at ten o'clock Anna was sitting at the back of the island's main church. She'd suggested she not come—this should be the islanders' dream rather than hers—but Carla had been adamant on that score as well.

'You can't give it away for twenty years and they know it. They need to accept you.'

'Will they ever?'

There was no answer, so all she could do was stay as inconspicuous as possible. As she waited for the service to begin Carla sought her out and

tried to drag her down the front but she was having none of it.

'Leo's mother?' she asked Carla.

'She's a little better,' Carla told her, her face
lighting up. 'I dropped by an hour ago. You
must have done her good last night. When I left
she was even saying she wanted to come here!
Today! I have no idea if that's possible, but Leo's
coming. He says he couldn't speak yesterday so
he wants to speak today. Anna, my son's down
at the front. Come and sit with us.'

'Please, no.'

So she was left. She'd found a seat in a nook
behind a pillar where she had to peer sideways
to see. The people around her cast her curious
glances but left her alone.

That was how life was for her. The islanders
were outwardly courteous, but always wary.

With no one to talk to she focussed instead on
her surroundings. The church was ancient, and
impressive.

'It was built for ceremonial occasions by the
Castlavarans,' Carla had told her, 'but it's been
neglected for generations as the Castlavarans
lost their faith and the islanders had no funds to
keep it up.'

It looked beautiful today, decorated with sheaves and sheaves of the island's wild roses, but the flowers barely disguised the need for repair.

How could she present restoration to the trustees, she thought. 'I need a church for my present happiness?'

And then the service started. It was a simple service, a blessing on what was being done, prayers of thankfulness for what had happened two weeks ago, hopes for what the medical service might mean to the islanders in the years ahead.

Might, she thought. *Might?* Still distrust.

And then Leo stood to speak.

The congregation had been a little restless, clearly there because they felt obligated to be but not ready to be too invested in what still might not come to pass. But the moment Leo stood, the stillness was absolute.

He had their absolute attention. Their absolute trust.

He should be the castle patriarch, she thought yet again.

And then he spoke, quietly, strongly, well. He

spoke of a long-ago dream. He spoke of the near miracle of what he saw happening. He spoke of his hopes for what Anna was doing, of his pride in what had already happened, and his trust in what she was doing into the future.

He almost had her forgetting the distrust. He spoke simply, his emotion struggling to be contained. There was thankfulness in his voice, but also deep weariness. She could see it on his face, a man whose responsibilities had stretched him thin. This was a man who was there for every islander. A man who never turned from what had to be done.

Including the gut-wrenching decision not to take comfort in her body, not to let himself love her.

She knew it. As she sat there and watched, as she listened to what was indeed a personal thanks to her, she accepted their combined story for what it was—one of sacrifice. She'd been deeply hurt, but for Leo that pain must have been just as deep. There were so many things he'd given away.

She'd pressed Carla about Leo's love life once, and Carla had given a mirthless chuckle.

'Our Leo? When would he have time to do some courting? There are plenty of island girls who'd take him with joy, but his head's been taken up with the medical needs of this island.'

But it can't have been entirely, she thought. Not for all these years. She of all people knew how Leo responded to a woman, how much joy he'd found in her body. There must have been opportunities to marry one of his own.

One of his own. The phrase resonated as Leo finished outlining plans for the future, as he sought her face in the crowd and managed a smile, a smile of weariness and gratitude and acceptance, and as the congregation stood to sing.

One of his own. She wasn't one of 'his'. She was a Castlavaran.

But she wasn't.

Anger was suddenly her overriding emotion. A child's bad-tempered shout suddenly came to her, heard in some long-ago surgery when she was asking to see a spotty chest. *'No! Can't make me!'*

No one should be able to make her something she wasn't.

So what was she, then? A Raymond? Her mother

had married briefly, but the name was all she had of the man who'd fathered her. Her tentative approaches to meet him had been met with rebuffs.

So if she wasn't a Raymond and she wasn't a Castlavaran, then what?

Things were clearing. The resentment she'd held for so many years was gone and in its place...determination.

Donna's words hung over her. *'If I could see a way...'*

Would there ever be a better time?

Would she ever feel this brave again?

And before she could change her mind she started moving out toward the aisle. She had to edge her way past a sea of curious islanders to reach it.

Leo was still standing beside the priest. The priest looked curiously down the aisle as he felt the stir of movement. He saw Anna.

And Leo... He, too, stood still.

Waiting.

Dear heaven, could she do it?

She had this one chance, she thought. If not now, then never.

'Help me, Donna,' she whispered to herself. 'Help me say it.'

* * *

For Leo this felt almost like an out-of-body experience.

He'd sat last night with his mother, half expecting her to slip away in the night. Then Anna had come and Donna had stirred and demanded answers to questions he'd rather not think about. And then she'd demanded he dress her and carry her to the church.

And astonishingly she was here now, wrapped in blankets, surrounded by his aunts and cousins. They'd appropriated a nook to one side so Donna could watch and listen from her wheelchair. When he'd come forward to speak he'd been aware that his mother's eyes were bright and inquisitive, seemingly more alive than he'd seen them for months.

She couldn't last much longer. Her body weight…her fluid intake…impossible. But that she was here this morning was a miracle.

And now here was Anna.

She should have been seated in the front pew. He'd thought that as he'd entered and seen her, far up the back, trying to be invisible.

She'd be feeling that she had no place here.

He'd helped her feel that way, and he hated it. But as he looked around the sea of faces in the congregation, out to where his mother sat, once again came the knowledge that his way had been right. It was still right.

In time, given the medical services they deserved, the islanders could come to depend on him less, shifting loyalty to a myriad of other places. But for now he was still the Doctor. The man who'd persuaded them to have their children vaccinated, to eat less salt in their diets, to stop putting honey on their babies' pacifiers. He was the man they'd helped educate, who they'd supported to be here for them in times of trouble. The man they still needed to trust.

The man who'd had to turn away from his need of Anna.

But now Anna was out in the aisle, making her way steadily toward the front.

Toward him.

The entire church seemed to take a collective breath.

Anna had dressed conservatively in a soft grey suit and white blouse. Her curls were caught back into a demure knot. Her outfit was entirely appropriate for this community where women of a certain age still covered their heads.

It'd be a crime for Anna to cover her head, he thought inconsequentially. It was even a shame that her hair was confined to a knot. Those blazing curls deserved to be free.

Free. The word seemed to stick in his head and stay.

She wasn't free. Because of her commitment to the island she was trapped in the castle as surely as he was trapped in his lifestyle. If she walked away she could still command living expenses, she'd still be fabulously wealthy, but she couldn't justify all the things she was doing 'for her pleasure'. The things she was doing to make his island safe.

She'd reached him now. He'd taken the two steps down from the altar and for a moment he thought she intended to walk past him. Her eyes looked steely, determined. He wasn't sure what she was doing but by her position on this island no one would gainsay her right to do it.

But instead of stepping past, she paused and placed a hand on his arm. It was almost a caress.

No, it *was* a caress, and why it grounded him... why it made his world seem to settle...

'Stand by me,' she said simply. 'Leo, I need you.'

And she took the final steps upward to the dais, leaving him to follow or not. As he willed.

The congregation was all islanders. That was where he belonged. But he looked back at her and saw determination and resolution. But also something more. A deep vulnerability, a hurt that had never been assuaged.

He stepped back to her.

She met his gaze without smiling and nodded, and then they both stood and faced outward. He stood so their shoulders were touching, not sure where this was going but suddenly sure that this was where he needed to be.

He watched her bite her bottom lip, a gesture he knew well. The gesture of a woman about to launch herself into the unknown.

And then she spoke.

'I ask your indulgence,' she said softly. 'The indulgence of all of you. Father, do I have your permission to speak?'

The elderly priest spread his hands, looking

bemused, but he nodded. No one said no to the Castlavaran.

Anna bowed her head briefly in thanks, and then continued while Leo stood, stunned. He had no idea what was happening.

But now she was speaking to the congregation.

'I had no plans to speak today,' she said. Her voice was quiet but steady, and the acoustics of this ancient place meant it rang out over the sea of listeners. 'I felt I had no right. This medical centre should belong to you, the islanders, not to me. I see myself simply as its guardian for the next few years.'

There was a murmur at that, and it wasn't a great murmur. It was the sound of muted resentment that such a guardian was needed.

But Anna wasn't done. Indeed, those first few words seemed to have steadied her. She waited until the murmurs faded and then continued.

'But what I have to say now concerns that guardianship,' she said simply. 'It concerns all of us, so I ask your indulgence.' She took a deep breath and forged on.

'Last night I sat with Donna Aretino,' she told them. She glanced outward then at the sea of faces—and Leo saw her shock as she realised that Donna was here. But somehow she managed to smile at Donna and then she kept right on speaking.

'Most of you realise how ill Donna's been,' she told them. 'And last night, sitting with Donna, I saw things clearly, things that affect me, that affect you, that affect the island life that Donna represents. So at this time, at this blessing of all we intend to do, I need to ask a question. A question of all of you. First, though, a story.'

She had them all. The murmurs had gone. Every gaze was fixed firmly on the woman by Leo's side.

'You know that Katrina, my mother, was born a Castlavaran.' She was keeping it simple, keeping it slow. 'She left this island because she hated what her father and her brother were doing, but her grief at leaving Tovahna was profound. She married my father, an Englishman. I was born as Anna Raymond and my mother never spoke of Tovahna again. In my childhood, though, she taught me what she called her secret language. Your language. She sang me your songs. Her love of this island came through. And then at medical school I met a man who spoke your language as well. This man was your Dr Aretino. And I fell in love.'

Somewhere up the back of the church a baby gurgled but the gurgle was cut short. The hush that followed was absolute. Leo wondered what the mother had done to so skilfully quieten her child. Every ear was straining to hear, his own included.

What was she doing?

'And your Dr Leo loved me.' She said it strongly, surely, and he knew by the steadiness of her voice that ten years of bitterness and resentment had disappeared. 'We had six glorious months together before he asked me to marry him and I said yes. But then my mother returned from overseas and Leo realised who she was. A Castlavaran. From that moment I became a Castlavaran in Leo's eyes. I know now the damage the Castlavarans have done to this island. I know, too, the damage they've done to Donna, to this gentle lady who, miraculously it seems, is here today. I also know the hurt they've caused to Leo himself. I understand why he had to walk away from our vow to wed.'

There was another stir then. This was news to the islanders. A long-ago love affair... Leo looked out over the congregation and saw the faint withdrawal. They didn't like this. The connection of a man they'd trusted...

Trusted...past tense?

Anna must have sensed it, too, he thought, but she was forging on. He was still standing beside her, his shoulder still touching hers. As the stirrings of distrust began he thought maybe he should step away but he couldn't. What she was saying was truth, and on this day, in this place, there seemed no space for anything else.

'So Leo finished his training without me, and then came back here, to his people,' she continued. 'As you all know. He's given his heart to this island, to you, his community, and of course to you, Donna. To his family. Though after all this time maybe every islander is his family. The Aretinos have been islanders since time immemorial. They've been fishermen, farmers, parents, grandparents, friends, part of the fabric of Tovahna. There's been care and respect and love for generations. All the while, the Castlavarans have cared for no one but themselves—and here I am, seemingly a Castlavaran, with no place among you.'

That created another murmur, but this time

there was a tinge of confusion. Agreement, too, though. Anna *was* an outsider.

He felt her flinch. The flinch was tiny, momentary, but it was enough and he couldn't bear it. He took her hand and he held it.

That was a statement, too. The murmur this time was louder, more disapproving. He wanted to say something but it felt like a band across his chest was tightening. This was an impossible situation. It had been impossible for years. Nothing could change it.

Except he was holding Anna's hand. He should let go but he couldn't. There were moments in time when the impossible became inevitable. There'd be consequences, he thought, but quite suddenly he knew that letting this woman go was the new unthinkable.

And Anna was still speaking. Her fingers curved around his and held on, as if finding strength there for what she wanted to say, but there was nothing weak about the voice she used, or the words she was uttering.

'But families change,' she said. 'Names die out. The name of Castlavara died with my uncle. There's no one of the name Castlavara on the island any more.'

'But you're the Castlavaran.' It was a brutish fisherman, a man in his seventies whose boat had been impounded decades before for drifting too close to the part of the beach that had been declared for Castlavaran use for centuries.

'I'm not.' Anna's voice rang back, strong but not angry. Simply sure. 'You know I was born a Raymond. My hair, my skin, are my father's, and my name is my father's. I do have, however, Castlavaran powers and for the next nineteen years there's nothing I can do about that.'

'You're doing all you can.' That was Carla, calling out from the front pew. 'You're giving us so much.'

'I'm not giving,' Anna said. 'I'm returning. And I want to return so much more. But you'll all know there's much I can't do. The Trust prevents it. In nineteen and a half years, though, the Trust will end and the island will pass into the control of the islanders. Your land will be your own. That's a promise I can make, I do make, but with Leo's help I can do so much more.'

'Like what?' It was the belligerent fisherman again.

'Like become one of you.' She spoke softly now, tentatively. Every islander had to strain to hear, but the acoustics of the church were such that each word still hung there. 'And that's what I need to be, an islander with islander concerns. The Trust says castle funds can be used for my comfort and enjoyment. That's how we got the castle medical centre. It's supposedly for my personal enjoyment because I'm a doctor, and how can I enjoy myself without a top-quality medical centre?

'But we need a home medical service as well, and how do I justify that to the Trust? We need good schools, a new harbour, sealed roads. We need transport for our olive crops. We need light industry, places where our fish, our olives can be processed so we can reap the profits. We need tourist infrastructure. We need jobs to stop our children leaving the island. We need so much.'

She turned then toward Donna, and for a moment she spoke only to that lady.

'Donna, you've worked hard and long for this island,' she told her. 'I've heard the stories. But overriding everything else, every decision you've taken was for your love of your family. For this island. And Leo's the same. His love for his father…the pain his death caused and the ripples of that spreading through his life… They've all helped to make him the man I know he is. He's devoted to you and to each and every person here. So that's why I'm standing here now. That's what I want for myself. Indeed, that's what I want for the whole island, and the thought of continuing without it is unbearable.'

She had them now. The blustering fisherman was looking at her through narrowed eyes. He was still suspicious, as surely every islander was suspicious—generations of mistrust couldn't be undone in a moment—but there was a collective waiting. *Wait and see...*

She glanced at Leo then, in her eyes a question, but her glance was fleeting, almost as if she was afraid of the answer she'd be given. And then she forged on.

'So here's my suggestion,' she said, and suddenly there was a tremor in her voice. The first sign of doubt? 'The Aretinos are a huge family. Leo is an only child but he has aunts, uncles, cousins, a family with members that must reach into almost every family on Tovahna. And because I love Leo, his concerns are my concerns. Donna, your concerns have become my concerns. Tovahna is becoming my family.'

But once again there was a moment when suspicion reigned. Leo was no longer sure where this was going but he saw the stillness, the closing of faces, the generations of mistreatment spreading its fog throughout.

But Anna saw it and faced it square on.

'That's why I'm here, now,' she said. 'If my family was a family such as the Aretinos, I'd love all my family and the Trust couldn't argue that my family's welfare wasn't a cause of my comfort and enjoyment. If my large and extended family can't access good schools, if my cousins can't fish safely, if the children of my family can't access good jobs…how can I be happy?'

They were starting to see it. There was the faintest lightening of expression on the sharpest of the islanders' faces.

Leo was before them. His grip on Anna's hand tightened still further and he tried to tug her to face him but she wouldn't have it. Her feet were planted squarely and her face spoke of determination to see this through to the end.

'Once upon a time Dr Leo Aretino asked me to marry him.' She was deliberately not looking at him, speaking only to the islanders. 'He turned away because of his love for this island. I've been here now for six months and I've learned to love it as well. Not only that, I've learned that my love for Leo hasn't faded.'

'So marry him.' It was Carla, of course it was Carla. 'Marry him, Anna. You have our blessing.'

'I have your blessing, Carla,' Anna said gently. 'But I need more. So this is what I'm saying. My mother was born a Castlavaran and she rejected the name. I was born a Raymond but that name means nothing to me. Now…what I want, what I believe Leo wants, and I hope… Donna, I hope you want it, too… What I believe the islanders *need* is for the name of Castlavara to be finally finished. Ended. And for the islanders to take over the island as they should. Legally we can't do that for nineteen years but do we need to wait that long? All it takes is a name change. All it takes is for one man to take one woman as his wife.'

'Anna…' It was too much. Leo broke his silence and tugged her around so she was facing him. 'What are you saying?'

'I'm asking,' she said simply. 'But not you, Leo, because you're too honourable, too worried about your islanders, your family. Your mother said to me last night… *"If I could see a way…"*

Those were her words, and I hope she'll back me up now. With her help, I'm seeing a way. So now I'm asking the islanders.'

She met his gaze full on. Something passed between them. Something good. Something sure. Something that could last…for ever?

She smiled, the faintest of smiles, and turned back to the congregation.

'Ten years ago Leo asked me to become an Aretino,' she told them. 'So I ask now, in Donna's presence, with the man I love beside me, in the presence of every islander who could be here today, would you accept me into Leo's family? Would you have Leo—and Donna, too, for the time she has left to us—come and live in our vast island castle? Live there we must for another nineteen years if we're not to break the Trust, but will you let us work from there for the good of the islanders? Would you have me marry this man and be an islander and—with our marriage—let the name Castlavara disappear for ever?'

Silence. Total silence.

The stillness seemed almost deafening. It went on and on, as each islander thought of what they'd just heard.

Then there were mutterings. Whispers. Nudging.

And then suddenly Carla was on her feet. 'Come on, you cowards, just do it,' she called.

And Donna, astonishingly strong, was calling from the side, 'My loves, you have my blessing.'

And then someone started to clap—and amazingly it was the belligerent fisherman. And then a child clapped, because maybe children clapped when they weren't sure if they should follow or not.

And what followed… Every single islander was on his or her feet and the applause was almost deafening. The priest was surging forward to bless them, smiling on this the most solemn of occasions.

And Leo was looking at this woman he loved with wonder. With disbelief.

With joy.

He kissed her. Of course he kissed her—and the thing was done. She'd come home. And then somehow he put her back, at arm's length and the look on her face said it all.

Yet still he asked.

'Anna, I deserted you ten years ago… Will you come back to me?'

'Truly, I don't think I've ever left.'

'So you'll still marry me?'

'It would be my honour.'

'Now?'

And the sounds around them seemed to still again, fading to nothing. There was just this man, this woman and all the love in the world between them.

'Oh, Leo…' She was half laughing, half crying. 'Of course I'll marry you. Yesterday if you want.'

And then she was back in his arms and he was turning to the priest, who looked bewildered at this spectacular turn of events.

'Father…'

And the elderly priest suddenly realised what was being asked. His bewilderment turned to a beam a mile wide.

'Yes, my son?'

'I know it's common for banns to be called,' Leo said. 'And for all sorts of formalities to take place before a wedding. But ten years ago I asked Anna Raymond to be my wife and she said yes. Would a ten-year engagement count as replacement for formalities? Would you marry us now?'

He turned back to Anna. 'If that's what you

want, my love? Could you bear to marry without the full bridal? Could you marry me right now?'

And she was laughing, hauling the tie from her hair so her curls sprang free. Tugging off her grey jacket and tossing it to the side.

'How can you doubt it?' she asked, and she smiled and smiled. Her face was bright with love and laughter. 'A wedding. Now? Why not? I have everything I need. I think.' But then she wrinkled her nose. 'Flowers, though? Every bride I've ever seen has flowers.' But her eyes were laughing and he knew that flowers or not, their wedding was a done deal.

But flowers happened. The priest headed purposely toward once of the wall sconces, lifted out one of the sheaths of wild roses and proceeded to wrap the stems in an embroidered cloth covering a side table. The cloth was possibly as ancient as the church itself, but the priest obviously had different priorities.

'Here, my daughter,' he said, and then he fixed Leo with a stern look. 'What else? Rings? Do we have rings?'

Only about a hundred were offered on the instant.

But Leo shook his head as offers came from

everywhere. He smiled at Anna and that smile, oh, it was just for her.

'I have two rings,' he told her. 'An engagement ring that was handed back to me ten years ago, and a wedding ring we bought at the same time. They've been in my wallet every moment since.'

They needed no more. They could do the legal formalities later.

'You have everything you need, then,' the priest said. 'If you're both sure...'

'We're sure,' they said in unison.

'Then let's do it,' the priest said, and smiled and smiled, and he turned back to the congregation. 'Dearly beloved...we are gathered here today...'

And thus they were married.

The vows were made. Leo took his bride out into the morning sunshine. Every rose in the church was stripped to produce petals to throw.

Anna hardly noticed, for Leo's hand held hers, and every islander knew that her hand would be in his for ever.

CHAPTER TWELVE

Nineteen and a half years later

THE PLANE WAS about to leave and Dr Anna Aretino was a sodden mess. She'd been sobbing since she'd woken this morning and her husband wasn't much better. Leo was just holding it together.

The two girls reached the top of the plane steps and turned to wave. These were the Aretino twins, non-identical, one a dark-haired beauty, the other redheaded, vivacious, gorgeous. The only thing identical about them was their smiles, both a mile wide.

'I can't believe they're going.' Anna was tucked under Leo's arm, hugging and being hugged, sniffing into his oversized handkerchief.

'Mama, leave it off.'

At fifteen, Georg was showing every sign of being just as good looking as his father—once he lost the braces from his teeth. He was currently waving to his sisters, but he was also laughing at his parents.

'Look at you both. Your daughters have scholarships to the same medical school you went to. They're off to see the world. They're so happy they're practically sickening, and you know they'll be back at first term break—and the next term break—and the one after. And they're already planning careers here. You don't get rid of kids from this island. You know we'll always want to come back.'

Anna had a final sniff and returned the handkerchief to her husband's pocket. Her son was right, they would be back.

This island was home.

'And now it's time we did what we promised to do all those years ago,' Leo said softly. 'It's a shame the girls' term started so early they couldn't stay to see this through, but the rest of us... Come on, Georg. Ready, my love?'

She was ready. Georg was right, her daughters were launching themselves into the world and she should feel nothing but joy for them. On this day of all days, she should feel joy for all the island.

And in the end what followed was almost an

anti-climax. The lawyers' documents were ready to sign. Names, dates, signatures, witnesses and the thing was done.

Tovahna belonged to the people.

'Terrific,' Georg said in the tone of a long-suffering teenager who'd been dragged along to something that didn't interest him. 'Now can I go to football?'

So he was left at the football grounds and Drs Leo and Anna Aretino made their way back to the castle.

The castle was, after all, their home. Their massive apartment would stay in their name. A smallholding of beach-side farmland on the far side of the island—once worked by Leo's great-grandfather—was also retained. The rest was either transferred to the islanders whose home it was, or held as public property to be administered by the island council.

The battlements of the castle were thus no longer Anna's property but they hadn't been used as such for years. They were now, and into perpetuity, available to the patients, residents, staff of Tovahna's world-class medical centre.

For this day, though, it had been decreed that for one last time the battlements would revert to being Leo and Anna's own space. They'd asked for privacy and they had it.

So without children, without any encumbrances—apart from two doofus dogs because dogs had always been and would always be a part of their lives—they made their way to where they'd stood so long ago, looking out over the sea beyond their island home.

As they reached the parapets Leo took his wife into his arms and kissed her. It was a long, steadying kiss. It was a kiss that grounded them in the knowledge that what they had was wonderful. What they had was family, home and joy in spades.

'We've done it,' Anna murmured, when there was time and space to speak. 'Our family's launched onto a new and exciting path, and Tovahna finally belongs to our people.'

'*You've* done it,' Leo told her, kissing her ear. 'My lady of the castle. The last of the Castlavarans.'

'That's not who I am,' she said contentedly. 'I'm the wife of Dr Leo Aretino. I'm the mother of three gorgeous children. I'm the shared head of a dynasty of dumb dogs and I'm a family doctor to any islander who wants to use me. Castlavara? As of today it's a name that's forgotten. Leo, we have done right, haven't we?'

'I can't think of anything we could have done better,' he told her, and he kissed her again. 'Tomorrow the islanders will receive their land titles, but it hardly matters any more. You gave the island back to the people twenty years ago.'

'*We* gave it back. If I hadn't met you…if I hadn't fallen in love with you…'

'It doesn't bear thinking of,' he said. 'But now…we've asked for privacy for this one last time. Complete privacy. Are you thinking what I'm thinking?'

'Yes, but the windows…'

'I decreed that, too,' he said smugly. 'The battlements are to be ours for this final day, and the deal is that every window facing east shall have its blinds firmly drawn.'

'People will cheat,' Anna told him. 'If I was told to pull my blinds and not look then I'd cheat.'

'Then the islanders are about to be shocked.' Leo was already tugging her away from the parapets, down the stairs toward the beach below. 'Twenty years ago I swam almost naked with you, my love, and I almost made love to you. For twenty years I've been regretting that "almost".

After today the islanders have the right to be here any time they want, but today it's ours, my lady. So what do you say? A swim and whatever comes after?'

'What's happened until now has been wonderful enough,' she told him, smiling and smiling, and she was already unbuttoning her blouse as they headed downstairs.

'It was simply a forerunner,' Leo told her. He turned in the stairwell and tugged her back into his arms, to kiss her, hard and strong. 'A family, an island, a nation… Why do I believe the best is yet to come?'

And then they reached the beach. Their clothes were gone. They dived into the sapphire water and started the long swim out to 'their' rock.

And if the islanders were shocked, then that was their problem, because Leo's belief was proven most definitely right.

* * * * *

LET'S TALK

For exclusive extracts, competitions and special offers, find us online:

f facebook.com/millsandboon

⃝ @millsandboonuk

🐦 @millsandboon

Or get in touch on 0844 844 1351*

For all the latest titles coming soon, visit millsandboon.co.uk/nextmonth

*Calls cost 7p per minute plus your phone company's price per minute access charge